中国南方著名古典史诗英译丛书

丛书主编　张立玉　起国庆

阿昌族、德昂族古典史诗

（汉英对照）

兰克　杨智辉　陈志鹏　整理

张立玉　臧军娜　英译

[美] H.W. Lan　审校

出品单位：

中南民族大学南方少数民族文库翻译研究基地

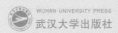

WUHAN UNIVERSITY PRESS

武汉大学出版社

图书在版编目(CIP)数据

阿昌族、德昂族古典史诗 = Classical Epics of Achang and De'ang：汉英对照／兰克，杨智辉，陈志鹏整理；张立玉，臧军娜英译.--武汉：武汉大学出版社，2024.8.--中国南方著名古典史诗英译丛书／张立玉，起国庆 主编.--ISBN 978-7-307-24500-6

Ⅰ.I222.7

中国国家版本馆 CIP 数据核字第 20240PA666 号

责任编辑:李晶晶　　　责任校对:鄢春梅　　　版式设计:韩闻锦

出版发行:**武汉大学出版社**　（430072　武昌　珞珈山）
　　　　　（电子邮箱:cbs22@whu.edu.cn　网址:www.wdp.com.cn）
印刷:武汉科源印刷设计有限公司
开本:720×1000　1/16　印张:14　字数:167千字　插页:1
版次:2024年8月第1版　2024年8月第1次印刷
ISBN 978-7-307-24500-6　定价:68.00元

丛书编委会

序

在千古悠悠的历史长河中，中华民族以自己的勤劳和智慧创造了光辉灿烂的古典史诗。古典史诗是一种结构庞大、富有综合性特征的民间长篇叙事诗，一般分为创世史诗、英雄史诗和迁徙史诗三大类，其内容丰富、气势恢弘，在漫长的传承过程中，融进了大量的民间神话、传说、故事、歌谣和谚语等，是一个民族社会生产活动、宗教信仰、风俗习惯和历史文化知识的一种特殊总汇。它经过长期的积累，深深积淀于中华民族的精神文化宝库之中，是千百年来中华民族自尊、自信、自爱、自强意识的重要源泉。它对中华民族文化传统的形成和发展产生了巨大而深远的影响。

近年来，为了推动中华文化的国际传播、提升中华文化的影响力、深入挖掘中华文化的精神内核、让中国优秀传统文化走出去，中南民族大学南方少数民族文库翻译研究基地积极对中国南方非遗文化典籍进行对外传播和译介的工作。该基地民族典籍英译捷报频传、硕果累累。先后出版了土家族典籍英译2部，纳西族三大史诗英译3部，"十三五"国家重点图书、国家出版基金项目"中国南方民间文学典籍英译丛书"14部。

近日，该翻译研究基地又传来佳音：他们要出版"中国南方著名古典史诗英译丛书"。这套丛书包括十余本，分别是《苗族古歌》《巴塔麻嘎捧尚罗》《厘俸》《阿昌族、德昂族古典史诗》《阿黑西尼摩》《相勐》《阿细的先基》《白族古典史诗（上、下）》《拉祜族创世史诗》《傈僳族叙事诗》《德傣掸登俄》。这些典籍多数入围了国家级非物质文化遗产名录，展示了不同民族的文化。

《苗族古歌》又称"大歌"，作为苗族的创世史诗，它是苗族口传文学的典型代表，也是记录苗族古代社会的一部百科全书。它于2006年5月20日被国务院批准列入第一批国家级非物质文化遗产名录。苗族的各种文化艺术都可以从这里找到它们的源头，《苗族古歌》的内容森罗万象，有苗族的发展史、远古时期的开天辟地、繁衍人类、耕耘劳作、衣食住行、婚丧嫁娶、重建家园，还有苗族人民长期遭受压迫和剥削而反抗以争取自由幸福的生活等内容。它不仅具有历史学、民族学、哲学、人类学的研究价值，还具有教育、审美和娱乐等方面的杰出价值；它是研究远古思想的形象化材料，是苗族历史的艺术写照，也是了解苗族社会习俗的窗口。

《巴塔麻嘎捧尚罗》为傣族创世史诗，是傣族文学的巅峰之作，也是我国南方少数民族创世史诗的经典之作。与《乌沙巴罗》《粘芭西顿》《兰嘎西贺》《粘响》一同被傣族人民称作"五大诗王"。《巴塔麻嘎捧尚罗》融合了傣族本土的神话叙事与外来的佛经叙事，经过历代歌手的不断演述以及文人创编成文、誊抄成本，逐渐实现书面化和系统化，最终形成了15000多行的长篇史诗。这部史诗内容宏大，包括天神英叭诞生、英叭开天辟地、众神诞生、地球毁灭又重生、布桑嘎西与雅桑嘎赛修补天地又捏土造人、葫芦孕育万物、天神制定历法、桑木底教人造屋定居、人类大兴旺、民族迁徙等内容。

《厘俸》是一部在傣族文学史上具有重大意义的英雄史诗，主要叙述了古代英雄海罕和俸改之间的战争，并展示了傣族先民从原始社会解体到奴隶制初期广阔的社会生活。《厘俸》是傣族文学史乃至文化史上一部具有里程碑意义的作品，是傣族形成和崛起期所有重大历史事件、军事行动、社会生活、时代风尚、英雄崇拜、信仰体系以及各种英雄传说的历史积淀和艺术创造的结晶。它具有民族史、民族学、宗教学、文化学、文艺学等多学科的价值，堪称傣族古代社会文化的"百科全书"，是一部不可多得的文化遗产。

《阿昌族、德昂族古典史诗》由阿昌族和德昂族两个民族的史诗组成。阿昌族古典史诗《遮帕麻和遮米麻》是流传于云南省德宏傣族景颇族自治州梁河县的传统民间文学，2006年5月被列入第一批国家级非物质文化遗产名录。《遮帕麻和遮米麻》产生于阿昌族早期，是一部讲述阿昌族先民为了感谢遮帕麻和遮米麻的创世之恩，以及补天缝地、降魔降妖等多次挽救人类的大恩大德的民间文学作品，涵括了创世神话、人类起源神话、洪水神话，也包含了人祖英雄神话。这部长诗同时也形象地反映了人类从母权制向父权制过渡的状况。德昂族古典史诗《达古达楞格莱标》是流传于云南省德宏傣族景颇族自治州的民间文学，2008年被列入第二批国家级非物质文化遗产名录，也是德昂族迄今发掘、整理并出版的唯一一部创世史诗。与其他民族的创世史诗不同，《达古达楞格莱标》情节单纯，始终以万物之源——茶为主线，集中地描写了这一人类和大地上万物的始祖如何化育世界、繁衍人类的神迹，并以奇妙的幻想将茶拟人化，提出人类来源于茶树、德昂族是茶树的子孙的独特观点。

《阿黑西尼摩》是彝族创世史诗，流传于云南省元阳县彝族地区。中文版由施文科、李亮文唱述，罗希吾戈、普学旺翻译，收入《云南少数民族古典史诗全集（上卷）》，并入选"中华大国学经典文库"。全诗由序歌、阿黑西尼摩生万物、人类的起源、天地开始分、叭依定历法、旱灾、洪水泛滥、天地生日、长寿和死亡、婚嫁的起源和演变、祭祀兴起等部分组成，是彝族典籍文化的重要组成部分，具有重要的文化价值和历史价值。该史诗中的"神谱"自成系统，内容丰富，幻想奇特，在阐释天地万物的起源方面独树一帜，对研究彝族原始文化，特别是母体崇拜以及人类母系文化，均具有重要价值。

《相勐》取材于傣族历史上部落战争的重大事件，真实地反映了傣族古代社会由部落林立到部落联盟直至最后形成统一的历史进程，展示了广阔的社会生活，塑造了各种英雄人物，显示了民族崛起期——英雄时代的民族精神。在艺术手法上，作品采用框架叙事结构，即以一个故事贯穿全诗，再以大故事套小故事，使情节的发展变化纷繁又紧扣中心。此外，作品语言清新、优美，充分体现出傣族传统诗歌的独特韵味。《相勐》以其特定的历史价值与艺术成就，被称为傣族最为成熟的一部英雄史诗。

《阿细的先基》是彝族支系阿细人的史诗、彝族四大创世史诗之一，由云南弥勒县西山一带的阿细人民口头流传，以固定的"先基调"演唱而得名。在表现形式上采用"先基调"进行演唱，往往通过对唱提问、对答的方式展开诗篇。句式一般为五言，但到了"求爱"等感情激烈的段落时，间用六言和长短句，以便于抒情。全诗分两部分。第一部分"最古的时候"叙述天地万物的起源和人类早期的生活习俗。第二部分"男女说合成一家"记叙阿细人独特的婚姻和风俗习惯。具有传承意义。

拉祜族创世史诗《牡帕密帕》是拉祜族宗教文化的核心部分之一。拉祜族以"卑咯斯"（Birec）为神，他被认为是宇宙的创造者。《牡帕密帕》记录了对卑咯斯的崇拜方式、神话故事以及人们对神灵的祭祀活动。在拉祜族的历史中，这部史诗被传唱和演绎了几百年，并以其独特的形式和内涵成为了拉祜族宗教文化的重要组成部分，被视为拉祜族文化的瑰宝，它记录了拉祜族的起源、神话传说、社会生活等内容。这一史诗的传承与发展是拉祜族文化的传承与发展的缩影。

其余几本书展示了白族、傈僳族等的风俗习惯、恋爱故事、斗争故事等。《白族古典史诗(上、下)》中的《串枝连》《青姑娘》《鸿雁传书》三部长诗是白族文化典籍。《串枝连》热情歌颂了一对白族青年的自由恋爱和他们的坚贞爱情，突出表现了白族人民对"指腹为婚"这一残酷的封建婚姻制度的反抗。《青姑娘》则通过反映旧社会一个童养媳的不幸遭遇，揭露和控诉了封建礼教对青年妇女的残酷迫害。《鸿雁传书》描写的是一对青年夫妻，丈夫出门谋生，远离家乡，二人分居两地，他们只有托鸿雁传书，互相倾诉思念之情。《白族古典史诗(上、下)》中的《出门调》主要流传在云南剑川、洱源、兰坪等县和丽江、九河等白族地区，这部叙述诗通篇用第一人称演唱。它集中描写了剑川木匠出门在外的悲苦生活。而《出门恋歌》虽然也描写了男主人公因生活所迫，不得已与心爱的人分离、外出讨生活的情节，但重点是讲述男女主人公从相知相恋到分离后相思成疾，最终欢喜重逢的故事。

《傈僳族叙事诗》中的《生产调》生动形象地反映了傈僳族人民日常的生产劳动，表现了他们勤劳、善良、友爱、互助的民族性格和美好的民族风尚。《盖房调》为傈僳族古老的传统调子，来源于傈僳族盖房子的劳动。它对傈僳族古老的盖房习俗、住房结构、盖房时的劳动场面均作了真实、细致的描绘，这对人们研究傈僳族的社会生活具有重要的参考价值。《种瓜调》流传于怒江傈僳族自治州的碧江、泸水、福贡、贡山等地的傈僳族人民中，是傈僳族口头诗歌中流传比较广、影响较深的作品，诗中所说的南瓜发芽、出苗、串藤、开花、结瓜，实际上指的是男女青年爱情的成长过程。

《德傣掸登俄》是壮族土僚支系中广为流传的一部创世史诗，由开天辟地、洪水淹天、土僚创世、星女下凡四个部分组成。第一部分的内容为：天地是罗扎、罗妞开辟出来的，万物是罗扎、罗妞制造成的；第二部分的内容为：洪水淹天之后，在葫芦里躲过劫难的两兄妹结为夫妻，传下了人种；第三部分的内容为：土僚先民种稻种棉，铸造铁器，创造了美好生活；第四部分的内容为：天上的星女下凡与罗傣结婚，犹如爱神，为此，每年三月初三，土僚都要祭祀星女。整部长诗共两千多行，绝大部分为五言体，叙事奇特、结构紧密、内容丰富、韵味十足，经常由长老在举办红、白喜事时或节日期间吟诵，颇受群众欢迎，现仍广泛流传于红河流域的壮族地区。

这些故事都很引人入胜，都很符合国家文化发展需求，向世人讲述中国故事、传播中华文化，并且讲述的是中国少数民族故事，充分体现了党和国家对各民族的关怀。这些典籍中折射出的文化多样性极大地丰富了世界文化，使世界文化更加丰富多彩、绚丽多姿。因此，民族典籍英译是传播中国文化、文学和文明的重要途径，是中华文化走出去的重要组成部分，是提高文化软实力的重要方式，在文化交流和文明建设中起着不可或缺的作用，对提高中国对外话语权和构建中国对外话语体系、对建设世界文学都有积极意义。

张立玉　起国庆

2023 年 12 月

前　　言

　　本书包括两个民族的古典史诗，分别为：阿昌族的《遮帕麻和遮米麻》和德昂族的《达古达楞格莱标》。

　　《遮帕麻和遮米麻》是流传于云南省德宏傣族景颇族自治州梁河县的传统民间文学，2006 年 5 月被列入第一批国家级非物质文化遗产名录，是阿昌族活袍在祭祀活动时唱诵的经诗，在阿昌族宗教和民俗活动当中，都要念诵全部的《遮帕麻和遮米麻》。"遮"在阿昌语中指"打仗的兵"，"帕麻"和"米麻"分别是对年长的男子和妇女的尊称，"遮帕麻"指军队首领和统帅，"遮米麻"是统帅的妻子。在阿昌族的文化和信仰中，遮帕麻与遮米麻享有极高的声誉，被尊称为"天公"和"地母"。

　　《遮帕麻和遮米麻》产生于阿昌族早期，乃阿昌族先民为了感谢遮帕麻和遮米麻的创世之恩，以及补天缝地、降魔降妖等多次挽救人类的大恩大德而产生的一种民间文学，涵括了创世神话、人类起源神话、洪水神话，也包含了人祖英雄神话。这部创世长诗同时也形象地反映了人类从母权制向父权制过渡的状况。故事中的盐婆神话是古代西南民族游牧文化的一块"活化石"。《遮帕麻和遮米麻》是阿昌族文化发展的一座丰碑，阿昌族将其称为"我们民族的歌"。

　　《遮帕麻和遮米麻》全诗长 1600 余行，除了序歌外，分为四个部分。第一部分"创世"，讲述远古时候没有天，也没

1

有地，是天公"遮帕麻"造天，地母"遮米麻"织地，人类才逐渐繁衍，其包括"遮帕麻造天""遮米麻织地""天公地母传人种"三部分。第二部分"补天治水"，讲述遮帕麻和遮米麻为了世间万物的生存，战胜洪水灾难，包括"遮米麻补天""遮帕麻造南天门"两部分。第三部分"妖魔乱世"，讲述旱神"腊訇"造了个假太阳，钉在天幕上，毁灭了人类的幸福，包括"腊訇作乱""水獭猫送信""遮帕麻回归"三部分。第四部分"降妖除魔"，讲述遮帕麻和遮米麻降妖除魔、制伏腊訇，用神箭射落假太阳，使人类获得新生，包括"斗法""斗梦""智伏腊訇""重整天地"四部分。《遮帕麻和遮米麻》整部史诗内容丰富生动，各章节紧密相连，情节生动感人，人物性格鲜明，语言朴素清新。

史诗《遮帕麻和遮米麻》由阿昌族的活袍在特定的宗教仪式和民俗活动中念诵。阿昌族的"活袍"，译成汉语，就是"高级祭司"。活袍大多学识渊博，阅历丰富，懂医术，会治病。在阿昌族的日常生活中，活袍具有崇高的社会地位。阿昌族的宗教活动都有活袍参加，葬礼也多由活袍主持。凡是活袍参加或主持的活动，都要由活袍诵经，而活袍所诵经文，主要是史诗《遮帕麻和遮米麻》。

在阿昌族最大的民族节日及阿昌族最大的民俗活动"阿露窝罗节"中，阿昌族人们通过跳"蹬窝罗"舞蹈来歌颂始祖遮帕麻和遮米麻创造人类、繁衍子孙以及不屈不挠的斗争精神。阿昌族的泼水节，又称桑建节，也源于神话《遮帕麻和遮米麻》。普通百姓在修建房屋、迎候亲戚、娶亲迎候媒人的时候，都要一边唱歌一边跳舞，唱颂阿昌族的始祖遮帕麻和遮米麻创造了人类，从而让族人之间可以联姻并不断地繁衍生息。遮帕麻和遮米麻不仅是阿昌族最受崇拜的至尊善神，而且也是所有寻常人家的护佑之神和阿昌族祭祀活动的主掌之神。

　　本次英译采用的汉语版源于云南人民出版社 2009 年出版的《云南少数民族古典史诗全集》(中卷)，阿昌族人赵安贤演唱，杨叶生汉译，兰克、杨智辉整理版本。在英译中我们尽量保存其朴素清新的表达，力图再现原文展现的排比、夸张、比兴、比喻、拟人等修辞手法及阿昌族文化信息和独特民族特色。这部创世史诗中形象生动的叙事描述及人物刻画使读者和听者脑海里浮现的史诗画面栩栩如生。在翻译过程中，译者主要采用直译和音译方式，为保留原诗中的独特语言和生动比喻，尽量还原其语言特色和文化韵味。

　　《达古达楞格莱标》是流传于云南省德宏傣族景颇族自治州的民间文学，2008 年被列入第二批国家级非物质文化遗产名录，也是德昂族迄今发掘、整理并出版的唯一一部创世史诗。在德昂语中，"达古"和"达楞"是祖先的称谓(有些文献又称"达楞""亚楞"，部分德昂族知名人士和学者倾向后者)，"格莱标"就是德昂族祖先们的传说，"达古达楞格莱标"，德昂语意为"最早的祖先传说"。

　　与其他民族的创世史诗不同，《达古达楞格莱标》情节单纯，始终以万物之源——茶叶为主线，集中地描写了这一人类和大地上万物的始祖如何化育世界、繁衍人类的神迹，并以奇妙的幻想将茶拟人化，独特地提出人类来源于茶树、德昂族是茶树的子孙的观点。德昂人祖祖辈辈都把茶树视作具有生命、意志和伟大能力的对象而加以崇拜：是茶叶战胜了恶魔，是茶叶撵走了洪水，是茶叶兄妹用他们的皮肉装扮了大地，是茶叶兄妹达楞和亚楞留在人间，历经重重磨难，繁衍了人类。

　　《达古达楞格莱标》全诗长 1200 余行，除了序歌外，分为五个部分。第一部分"茶神下凡诞生人类"，讲述智慧神帕达然的出现及茶树如何创造了日月星辰。小茶树不顾智慧神帕达然的警告来到人间，它身上的 102 片茶叶在空中转了三万年，化成 102 个青年男女。第二部分"光明与黑暗的斗争"，讲述 102 个茶叶兄妹来到人间后，遭受各种磨难，最终在日月星辰的帮助下，渡过了难关。第三部分"战胜洪水和恶势力"，讲述茶叶兄妹为驱赶洪水，把自己的身子和眼泪化为高山、平坝和江河湖海。第四部分"百花百果的由来与腰箍的来历"，讲述茶叶兄妹撕碎自己的皮肉撒在地上变成百花，及藤篾箍习俗的来历。第五部分"先祖的诞生和各民族的繁衍"，讲述达楞和亚楞的子孙，为了传颂祖先的恩德，发明了"葫芦笙""吐良""口弦""象脚鼓""铓""镲"等乐器，以表达对祖先的缅怀、感恩。《达古达楞格莱标》是德昂族心中的历史，对人们的行为规范有重要指导作用，体现着德昂族的民族精神和人文思想，具有历史学、文化学、民俗学和伦理学等诸多方面的研究价值。

《达古达楞格莱标》内容充实，情节丰满曲折，扣人心弦，语言优美传神，音韵和谐。诗中还充满了奇特的想象，运用夸张手法，造成了一种人与超人间交替的意境。虽然不是长诗，却是一幅绚丽多姿的艺术长卷，储存着大量德昂族远古历史的信息，也成功地营造了一个瑰奇雄伟的美学境界。

本次英译采用的汉语版源于云南人民出版社 2009 年出版的《云南少数民族古典史诗全集》（中卷），德昂族人赵腊林唱译，陈志鹏记录整理。在译文中我们尽量保存其传神优美的语言，力图再现原文想象、夸张、比兴、比喻、拟人、排比等修辞手法及德昂族文化信息和独特民族特色。这部创世史诗中传神的故事情节及人物刻画使读者和听者脑海里浮现的史诗画面奇特瑰丽。在英译过程中，译者主要采用直译和音译方式，为保留原诗中的独特语言和丰富的想象，尽量还原其语言特色和和谐韵味。

　　翻译过程中译者多次与担任审校工作的美国威斯康星大学拉克罗斯分校英语系的 Haixia W. Lan 教授深入交流讨论，并得到她的悉心指导。为了尽量理解和再现原文本中所包含的生态语境，译者还进行了大量的文献研究和实地调研，希望尽量减少误读与误译，力求英译忠实原文，并传递阿昌族的语言和文化。由于译者水平有限，翻译过程中难免有疏漏之处，恳请广大读者朋友批评指正，以便修订时更正。

张立玉　臧军娜
2023 年 12 月于南湖书斋

目　　录

上篇：遮帕麻和遮米麻

下篇：达古达楞格莱标

Contents

Part 1：Zhepa Ma and Zhemi Ma

Part 2: Earliest Dagu and Daleng Legends

上篇：
遮帕麻和遮米麻

Part 1:
Zhepa Ma and Zhemi Ma

序　　歌

阿昌的子孙啊，
你记不记得阿公阿祖走过的路？
你知不知道我们阿昌的历史？
你晓不晓得造天织地的天公和地母？

晓不得大树的年轮算不得好木匠。
不会数牙口算什么赶马人？
不懂法术就做不了活袍。
晓不得祖宗怎么献家神？

我是一个老倌人，
故事是先辈传下来的。
造天织地的故事像流水一样，
传了千万代才传到我们这里。

静静地听吧，子孙们，
我来为你们歌唱，
让遮帕麻和遮米麻的故事，
像大盈江水一样长流不断。

Prelude

Ah, the offspring of Achang,

Do you remember the paths Grandpa and Great-grandpa walked?

Do you know the history of us Achang?

Do you know the heaven-building god and earth-weaving goddess?

Not knowing the rings of big trees one can't be a good carpenter.

What is a horseman who does not know how to count the horse's teeth?

Without knowing divination, one cannot be a high priest.

How can one offer sacrifice to the ancestor without knowing them?

I am a senior singer,
who tells stories passed down from elder generations.
The creation story is like the flowing water,
running generations after generations before reaching us.

Listen quietly, my children and grandchildren,
listen to me singing the story to you,
to make the legend of Zhepa Ma and Zhemi Ma
pass down like the rivers flowing continually.

第一部分 创世

在太古的时候没有天，
在太古的时候没有地。
整个的世界混沌不分，
不会刮风也不会下雨。

造天的是天公，
天公就是遮帕麻；
织地的是地母，
地母就是遮米麻。

今天是个好日子，
我给你们讲故事：
先讲遮帕麻造天，
再讲遮米麻织地。

Chapter One   Creating the World

There had not always been the sky,
nor had there always been the earth.
Before the heaven and earth there was chaos
with neither the wind nor the rain.

It was the heaven god who built the sky,
and this god of the sky is Zhepa Ma;
it was the earth goddess who wove the earth,
and this goddess of the earth was Zhemi Ma.

Today is a good day,
the day I shall tell you the story:
the story of Zhepa Ma building the heaven
before that of Zhemi Ma waving the earth.

第一折　遮帕麻造天

造天的是遮帕麻，
他没有裤子也没有衣裳，
只有一根神奇的赶山鞭，
系在腰杆上。

遮帕麻造天的时候，
带领着三十员神将，
跟随着三十名神兵，
三千六百只白鹤飞来帮忙。

三十名神兵挑来银色的沙，
三十员神将担来金色的沙，
三千六百只白鹤列队飞，
衔来圣洁的仙水拌泥巴。

来到天空的正中央，
遮帕麻在手心里捏泥团：
用闪闪的银沙造月亮，
拿灿灿的金沙造太阳。

I. Zhepa Ma Building the Sky

The sky was built by Zhepa Ma
who had neither pants nor clothes
but one magical mountain-driving whip
fastening on his waist.

When Zhepa Ma made the sky,
he was leading thirty heavenly generals,
followed by thirty heavenly soldiers,
and three thousand and six hundred white cranes came to
their assistance.

He had the thirty heavenly soldiers to bring the silvery sand,
the thirty heavenly generals to carry over the golden sand,
and the three thousand and six hundred white cranes
forming a line
to bring the mystic water with their mouths for mixing the
mud putty.

When reaching the center of the sky,
Zhepa Ma rolled the mud balls in the palms:
with the sparkling sands of silver, he made the moon,
and with the glittering sands of gold, he created the sun.

遮帕麻造的月亮，
像一抔水清汪汪；
遮帕麻造的太阳，
像一塘火亮堂堂。

遮帕麻用右手扯下左乳房，
左乳房变成了太阴山；
遮帕麻用左手扯下右乳房，
右乳房变成了太阳山。

（天公遮帕麻啊，
舍去了自己的血肉；
今天的男人没有乳房，
就是因为这个缘故。）

遮帕麻用泥巴包住太阳，
太阳还是烫。
一千六百只白鹤衔来仙水，
洒在火辣辣的太阳上。

遮帕麻张开右边的胳膊，
夹起光闪闪的月亮；
遮帕麻伸出左边的胳膊，
夹起火辣辣的太阳。

The moon made by Zhepa Ma
was like water, pure and bright;
the sun made by Zhepa Ma
was like fire, luminous and alight.

He tore off his left breast with his right hand,
and the left breast turned into the Taiyin [moon] Mountain;
he pulled off his right breast with his left hand,
and the right breast turned into the Taiyang [sun] Mountain.

(Ah, the heaven god, Zhepa Ma,
sacrificed his own blood and flesh;
it is the reason
men nowadays have no breasts.)

When Zhepa Ma wrapped the sun with the mud putty,
the sun was still burning hot.
One thousand and six hundred white cranes brought mystic
water
and sprinkled it onto the hot sun.

Stretching out the arm on the right,
Zhepa Ma picked up the glittering moon;
stretching out the arm on the left,
Zhepa Ma picked up the burning sun.

迈步踩出一条银河，
跳跃留下一道彩虹，
吐气变作大风、白雾，
流汗化作暴雨、山洪。

遮帕麻举起月亮，
放到太阴山上；
遮帕麻举起太阳，
放到太阳山上。

月亮像一池清水，
吐着银光。
太阴山上设下白银宝座，
派勾娄早芒掌管。

太阳像阿昌人的火塘，
散发着温暖。
太阳山上设下黄金宝座，
派毛鹤早芒掌管。

遮帕麻找来一棵梭罗树，
种在太阴山和太阳山中间。
告诉勾娄和毛鹤：
太阴和太阳要绕梭罗树旋转。

He walked to leave behind a Milky Way,
leaped to form a rainbow,
breathed to produce the gales and fog,
and sweated to cause storms and floods.

Zhepa Ma raised the moon
and put it on the Taiyin [moon] Mountain;
Zhepa Ma raised the sun
and put it on the Taiyang [sun] Mountain.

The moon was like a pond of water,
emitting silver light.
He set a silver throne on the Taiyin Mountain
and asked god Goulou to oversee it.

The sun was like Achang people's fire pit,
sending forth warmth.
He set a gold throne on the Taiyang Mountain,
and asked god Maohe to oversee it.

Zhepa Ma found a Reevesia tree
and planted it between the Taiyin and Taiyang Mountains.
He told god Goulou and god Maohe:
Taiyin and Taiyang should rotate around the Reevesia tree.

遮帕麻在梭罗树下忙碌，
造出一座星宿山，
山上安了一个大轮子，
派白鹤推着轮子转。

太阴出来是夜晚，
太阳出来是白天。
月亏月圆分月份，
轮转一圈是一年。

遮帕麻挥舞赶山鞭，
甩出火花一串串。
火花飞到云天里，
变成星宿亮闪闪。

遮帕麻造了东边的天，
东天设下琉璃宝座。
派茫鹤早芒住在东边，
让他把东边的天管着。

东边的天啊，
像清水一样清清吉吉；
东边的天啊，
像泉水一样清澄见底。

Zhepa Ma got busy under the Reevesia tree

and created Mount Constellation,

on which he fixed a large wheel

and sent the white cranes to push and keep it turning.

When Taiyin [the moon] came out, it was the night,

and when Taiyang [the sun] came out, it was the day.

When the moon had waned and waxed once, it was a month,

and [when the sun had rotated] a circle, it was a year.

Zhepa Ma swung the mountain-driving whip,

training of sparks flying out.

The sparks flew into the sky,

constellations rising twinkling high.

After Zhepa Ma created the sky in the east,

he set up a glass throne.

He then sent god Manghe to live in

and to oversee it.

Oh, the sky in the east

was as pure as the clear water;

oh, the sky in the east

was as clear as the spring water.

遮帕麻造好了南边的天，
南天设下莲花宝座。
派腊各早列住在南方，
让他把南边的天管着。

南边的天啊，
像清水一样清清吉吉；
南边的天啊，
像泉水一样清澄见底。

遮帕麻造好了西边的天，
西天设下玉石宝座。
派字劭早芒住在西边，
让他把西边的天管着。

西边的天啊，
像清水一样清清吉吉；
西边的天啊，
像泉水一样清澄见底。

遮帕麻造好了北边的天，
北边的天设下翡翠宝座。
北边的天空最尊贵，
派毛弥早芒管着。

After Zhepa Ma created the sky in the south,
he set up a lotus throne.
He then sent god Lage to live in
and to oversee it.

Oh, the sky in the south
was as pure as the clear water;
oh, the sky in the south,
was as clear as the spring water.

After Zhepa Ma created the sky in the west,
he set up a jade throne.
He then sent god Boshao to live in
and to oversee it.

Oh, the sky in the west
was as pure as the clear water;
oh, the sky in the west,
was as clear as the spring water.

After Zhepa Ma created the sky in the north,
he set up an emerald throne.
The northern sky being the most dignified,
he ordered god Maomi to oversee it.

北边的天啊，
像清水一样清清吉吉；
北边的天啊，
像泉水一样清澄见底。

遮帕麻造好了天的中央，
遮帕麻定下了天的四极；
勾娄毛鹤管日月，
毛弥早芒管天地。

遮帕麻造的天，
存在了万万年。
遮帕麻的功绩，
留在阿昌人的心坎。

遮帕麻造的日月，
光辉洒满大地。
遮帕麻的名声，
流传了千万个世纪。

Oh, the sky in the north
was as pure as the clear water;
oh, the sky in the north
was as clear as the spring water.

After Zhepa Ma created the center of the sky,
he set up the four different poles of the sky.
God Goulou and god Maohe oversaw the sun and the moon,
and god Maomi, the sky and the earth.

The heaven created by Zhepa Ma
has existed for thousands and thousands of years.
Zhepa Ma's achievements
have stayed in the heart of the Achang people.

The sun and the moon created by Zhepa Ma
have shined upon the whole earth.
Zhepa Ma's reputation
has spread for tens and thousands of centuries.

第二折　遮米麻织地

世界上有阴就有阳，
世界上有天要有地。
遮帕麻造天的时候，
遮米麻就开始织地。

她摘下喉头当梭子，
她拔下脸毛织大地。
（从此女人没有了胡须，
从此女人没有了喉结。）

遮米麻拔下右腮的毛，
织出了东边的大地。
东边的地像清水一样清清吉吉，
东边的地像泉水一样清澄见底。

遮米麻的右腮流下了鲜血，
淹没了东边的大地。
东边出现了一片汪洋，
化成东海无边无际。

东海波涛连天，
满是虾、鱼、龟、鳖。
东海里设下水晶宝座，
派东海龙王把它管理。

II. Zhemi Ma Weaving the Earth

As long as the world has the yin, it has the yang,
and as long as there is sky, there is earth.
When Zhepa Ma was making the sky,
Zhemi Ma was weaving the earth.

She removed her own throat as the shuttle
and her own face hair to weave the ground.
(Since then, women have had no beard or
the throat knot.)

Zhemi Ma plucked out the hair on her right cheek
and wove the eastern earth.
The earth in the east was as clear as the pure water
and as limpid as the spring water.

The blood from Zhemi Ma's right cheek
flooded the eastern land.
A vast sea appeared in the east
and became the boundless Eastern Sea.

The waves of the Eastern Sea roared high
and were filled with shrimps, fish, turtles, and tortoises.
A crystal throne was set up there,
    and the Dragon King of the Eastern sea was ordered to
oversee it.

遮米麻拔下左腮的毛，
织出了西边的大地。
西边的地像清水一样清清吉吉，
西边的地像泉水一样清澄见底。

遮米麻的左腮流下了鲜血，
淹没了西边的大地。
西边出现了一片汪洋，
化作西海无边无际。

西海波涛连天，
满是虾、鱼、龟、鳖。
西海里设下珍珠宝座，
派西海龙王把它管理。

遮米麻拔下下颌的毛，
织出了南边的大地。
南边的地像清水一样清清吉吉，
南边的地像泉水一样清澄见底。

遮米麻的下颌流下了鲜血，
淹没了南边的大地。
南边出现了一片汪洋，
化成南海无边无际。

Zhemi Ma plucked out the hair on her left cheek
and wove the western earth.
The earth in the west was as clear as the pure water
and as limpid as the spring water.

The blood from Zhemi Ma's left cheek
flooded the land in the west.
A vast sea emerged in the west
and became the bondless Western Sea.

The waves of the Western Sea roared high
and were filled with shrimps, fish, turtles, and tortoises.
A pearl throne was set up there,
and the Dragon King of the Western Sea was ordered to
oversee it.

Zhemi Ma plucked out the hair on her chin
and wove the southern earth.
The earth in the south was as clear as the pure water
and as limpid as the spring water.

The blood of Zhemi Ma's chin
flooded the land in the south.
A vast sea emerged in the south,
becoming the boundless Southern Sea.

南海波涛连天，
满是虾、鱼、龟、鳖。
南海里设下珊瑚宝座，
派南海龙王把它管理。

遮米麻拔下额头的毛，
织出了北边的大地。
北边的地像清水一样清清吉吉，
北边的地像泉水一样清澄见底。

遮米麻的额头流下了鲜血，
淹没了北边的大地。
北边出现了一片汪洋，
化作北海无边无际。

北海波涛连天，
满是虾、鱼、龟、鳖。
北海里设下了玛瑙宝座，
派北海龙王把它管理。

遮米麻织就了大地，
用的是血肉的躯体。
世界有了依托啊，
万物有了生机。

The waves of the Southern Sea roared high

and were filled with shrimp, fish, turtles, and tortoises.

A coral throne was set there,

and the Dragon King of the Southern Sea was ordered to

oversee it.

Zhemi Ma plucked out the hair from her forehead

and wove the northern earth.

The earth in the north was as clear as the pure water

and as limpid as the spring water.

The blood of Zhemi Ma's forehead

flooded the land in the north.

A vast sea emerged,

forming the boundless Northern Sea.

The waves of the Northern Sea roared high

and were filled with shrimps, fish, turtles, and tortoises.

An agate throne was set up there,

and the Dragon King of the Northern Sea was ordered to

oversee it.

Zhemi Ma wove the earth

with her own flesh and blood.

Ah, the world was nourished,

and all things in it came to life.

遮米麻织的大地，
存在了万万年。
遮米麻的功绩，
留在阿昌人的心坎。

大地无边无际，
到处流传着遮米麻的名声；
大海深不见底，
怎么比得上遮米麻的恩情！

阿昌的子孙啊，晒谷的时候，
不要忘记了遮帕麻；
喝水的时候，
不要忘记了遮米麻。

The earth woven by Zhemi Ma
has existed for thousands and thousands of years.
Zhemi Ma's achievements
have stayed in the heart of the Achang people.

On the boundless earth,
the reputation of Zhemi Ma was spread everywhere;
even the bottomless oceans
cannot be compared to the depth of Zhemi Ma's kindness!

Ah, the offspring of Achang, when drying the grains,
don't forget Zhepa Ma;
when drinking the water,
don't forget Zhemi Ma.

第三折　天公地母传人种

有上必有下，
有天要有地。
地支撑着天，
天覆盖着地。

天刚造就，
地刚织完。
天公遮帕麻啊，
来到大地的东方。

天刚造就，
地刚织完。
地母遮米麻啊，
出现在大地的西方。

天幕高高张开，
大地平平展展。
天像一个大锅盖，
地像一个大托盘。

天也造得好，
地也织得好，
只是天小地大了，
天边罩不住地缘。

III. The Heaven God and Earth Goddess Planting the Seeds of People

As long as there is up, there is down,
and if there is heaven, there must be earth.
While the earth supports the sky,
the sky covers the earth.

The sky was just made,
and the earth was just woven.
Ah, the heaven god Zhepa Ma
appeared in the east of the earth.

The sky was just made,
and the earth was just woven.
Ah, the earth goddess Zhemi Ma
appeared in the west of the earth.

The sky's curtain opened up high,
and the earth expanded flat.
The sky looked like a large pot,
and the earth was like a large tray.

The sky was well made,
and the earth was well woven,
but the sky was too smaller
to cover the edges of the earth.

遮帕麻拉拉东边的天，
西边的大地裸露了；
遮帕麻拉拉南边的天，
北边的大地裸露了。

拉天拉出滚滚雷，
雷声震天涯。
雷响三百里，
惊动了遮米麻。

遮米麻抽去三根地筋，
大地皱得像阿昌姑娘的筒裙。
凸的地方变成了高山，
凹的地方便是山箐。

大地卷缩了，
就像晒干的虎皮；
大地缩小了，
天幕才罩住了地的四极。

遮米麻抽去地筋三根，
大地顿时颤抖了。
地震扯动了三千里，
惊动了遮帕麻。

When Zhepa Ma pulled the east edge of the sky,
the earth on the west was exposed;
when Zhepa Ma pulled the south edge of the sky,
the earth on the north was bare.

The pulling caused the rolling thunder
that shook the entire sky.
The thunder spread three hundred miles far
and disturbed Zhemi Ma.

Zhemi Ma removed three tendons of the earth,
and the earth wrinkled up like Achang girls' pleated skirts.
The top of the fold becoming the high mountain,
and the bottom of the fold becoming the valleys.

The earth shrank,
like the dried up tiger skin;
the earth became smaller,
so the sky's curtain covered the four poles of the ground.

Zhemi Ma removed three tendons of the earth,
and instantly the earth shook.
The quake reached three thousand *li* away,
alarming Zhepa Ma.

震动平息过后，
山山水水变得无比秀丽。
遮帕麻朝四面看看，
美丽的山河多么神奇。

山头开满栀子花，
朵朵白花似雪洒。
花丛中住着百灵鸟，
百灵鸟叫处种山茶。

山腰开满攀枝花，
枝枝花开像火把。
花树上住着白鹇鸟，
白鹇欢鸣好安家。

山脚绣泵遍地黄，
花中住着金凤凰，
绣泵花开等蜂采，
凤凰合鸣寻伙伴。

"是什么样的巧手把大地织就？
是什么样的巧手把大地打扮？"
遮帕麻要寻找地母，
把千山万水走遍。

After the vibration stopped,

the mountains and rivers became exceptionally charming.

Zhepa Ma looked around,

and was amazed by its charm.

The top of the mountain was full of gardenia,

all blossoming as white as the snow.

Among the flowers lived larks,

who planted the camellia wherever their songs were heard.

The mountainside was full of flowery vines,

all blossoming as bright as fire.

Among the vines lived the silver pheasants,

singing joyfully and living peacefully.

Everywhere at the mountain foot was the yellow hydrangea,

where the golden phoenixes,

like the hydrangea flowers waiting for bees,

sang together to find partners.

"What kind of dexterous hands wove the earth?

What kind of skillful hands dressed up the earth?"

Zhepa Ma wanted to find the earth goddess,

going through hundreds and thousands of mountains and

rivers.

天罩住了大地，
好像盖房子有了屋顶。
五光十色的天空，
使遮米麻高兴万分。

天上星星数不清，
月亮落山太阳升。
太阳落下天就黑，
太阳升起天就明。

"是谁拉开的天幕？
是谁安排的四极？"
没有太阳，月亮不发光；
不见天公，难解遮米麻心头的谜。

遮帕麻寻地母，
下深箐、上高山。
深箐喝泉水，
高山找食粮。

野味生肉充饥，
嫩叶竹笋作粮，
石洞深处藏身，
光滑石板做床。

When the sky covered the earth,
it was like the roof was put on the house.
The multicolored sky
made Zhemi Ma overjoyed.

Countless stars were in the sky,
and the sun was rising up as the moon was setting down.
The day was dark with the sun set
and was light with the sun up.

"Who lifted the sky's curtain?
Who arranged the four poles?"
Without the sun, the moon could not glow;
without seeing the god of heaven, Zhemi Ma was puzzled.

Zhepa Ma looked for the goddess of the earth,
going down deep valleys and up high mountains.
He drank the spring water in the deep valleys
and searched for food on the high mountains.

He satisfied his hunger with the raw meat,
ate tender leaves and bamboo shoots as his grains,
hid in the depths of the stone cave for safety,
and slept on the stone slab as his bed.

剥下树皮当盖头，
连起兽皮做衣裳。
藤子腰间系，
打着光脚板。

一个美好的日子，
遮帕麻来到了大地的中央。
潺潺的流水清悠悠，
凉凉的泉水亮汪汪。

遮米麻找天公，
下深箐、上高山。
深箐喝泉水，
高山找食粮。

山果野梨充饥，
鲜花雀蛋做粮，
树洞里面藏身，
大树枝桠当床。

折叠芭华当盖头，
编起石华做衣裳。
藤子腰间系，
打着光脚板。

He peeled off the tree bark and used as his quilt,
made clothes out of the animal skin.
With rattan tying on the waist,
he walked barefooted.

On a wonderful day,
Zhepa Ma came to the center of the earth.
The river murmured with clear water,
and the spring water sparkled brightly.

Zhemi Ma looked for the god of the heaven,
going down the valleys and up the mountains.
She drank the spring water in the deep valleys
and searched for food on the high mountains.

She satisfied her hunger with berries and wild pears,
ate fresh flowers and sparrows' eggs as her grains,
hid in the depths of the tree hole for safety,
and slept on the big branches as her bed.

She folded up banana leaves as the quilt,
and made clothes out of straws.
With rattan tying on her waist,
she walked barefooted.

一个美好的日子，
遮米麻来到了大地的中央
潺潺的流水清悠悠，
凉凉的泉水亮汪汪。

遮帕麻来了，
流水伴他把俄罗①唱；
遮米麻来了，
泉水映出她美丽的模样。

唱一曲欢乐的巴松昆②，
遮帕麻的笑脸像天空一样晴朗；
唱一曲热烈的巴套昆③，
遮米麻的眼睛像月光那样明亮。

小鸟在树上唱歌，
天公地母在树下相逢。
好听的话啊，
像山泉淙淙。

---

① 俄罗，同"窝罗"，是遮帕麻从天上带来的。在阿昌语中无具体实意，有"聚拢起来"的意思，被当地人引申为"舞蹈"，因舞蹈中多为蹬腿、蹬地的动作，因此人们便喜欢将其称为"蹬窝罗"，就是"聚在一起欢乐地跳舞"的意思。

② 阿昌古语，"窝罗调"的序曲之一，表演的第二个程序，更加跳跃、轻快。与"巴套昆"一样都是具有邀约的含义。

③ 阿昌古语，"窝罗调"的序曲之一，表演的第一个程序，一般唱得并不长，有种打破沉闷的气氛，打断客人瞌睡，约大家一起歌舞的含义。

On a wonderful day,

Zhemi Ma came to the center of the earth.

The river murmured with clear water,

and the spring water sparkled brightly.

Zhepa Ma came,

singing the Eluo① with the water as his accompaniment;

Zhemi Ma came,

with the spring water reflecting her beautiful looks.

A happy Basong Kun② was sung,

and Zhepa Ma smiled like the bright sky;

A warm Batao Kun③ was sung,

Zhemi Ma's eyes lit up like the bright moonlight.

While the birds were singing on the tree,

the heaven god and earth goddess met under it.

Ah, the nice words

sounded like the mountain spring's gurgling.

---

① Eluo, the same as "Woluo", brought from the sky by Zhepa Ma, has no specific meaning but "gathering up" in the Achang language, extended by the local people as "dance". As it was mostly danced with driving legs, pushing off the ground, so people tend to call it "Deng Woluo", meaning "dancing together and having fun".

② The ancient Achang language, one of the preludes of the "Woluo tone", the second program of the dance, is brisk with more jumping. Like "Batao Kun", it has the meaning of invitation.

③ Achang ancient language, one of the preludes of "Woluo tune", the first program of the dance, generally sung not very long, has the meaning of breaking the dull atmosphere, interrupting the guests' sleep, and inviting everyone singing and dancing together.

遮米麻说："你造的天真好。
没有你造的月亮,
夜里看不见道路,
就连夜莺也不敢歌唱。

"没有你造的太阳,
万物不会生长;
没有你造的天,
我织的大地一片黑暗。"

遮帕麻说："我造的天再好,
比不上你织的大地。
没有大地的支撑,
天空就会像云彩随风飘移。

"大地有巍峨的高山,
大地有辽阔的平原,
大地有肥美的坝子,
大地有宽阔的海洋。"

遮米麻说："山高没有打猎人,
林深没有砍柴人,
地阔没有种田人,
海宽没有捕鱼人。"

Zhemi Ma said: "The sky you made is wonderful.

Without the moon you made,

the road would not be seen at night,

and even the nightingale would not dare to sing.

"Without the sun you made,

tens and thousands of things would not grow;

without the sky you created,

the earth I woven would be dark."

Zhepa Ma said: "No matter how wonderful the sky I made is,

it cannot be compared to the earth you wove.

Without support of the earth,

the sky would be floating like clouds moving with the wind.

"The earth has towering mountains,

vast plains,

fertile land,

and wide oceans."

Zhemi Ma said: "There is no hunter though the mountains

are high,

no woodcutter though the woods are thick,

no farmer though the land is wide,

and no fisherman though the sea is broad."

遮帕麻说："世上有了造天的人，
世上有了织地的人；
天和地已经合拢，
我们为什么还不合在一起？

"让我们同在一眼井里打水，
让我们同在一座山上狩猎，
让我们同围一个火塘吃饭，
让我们同在一个窝里安身。"

遮米麻说："这要去问你的爹，
这要去问你的妈。
你爹同意才能成亲，
你妈同意才能成家。"

遮帕麻说："我没有爹，
我也没有妈，
要问就去问天吧，
看天意许不许我们成一家。"

遮帕麻指着磨盘说：
"我从东山滚磨盖，
你从西山滚磨底，
磨盖磨底合拢就成婚。"

遮米麻指着两座山说：
"我在北山烧柴火，
你在南山烧柴火，
两山火烟相交我们就结合。"

Zhepa Ma said: "The world has the one who made the sky
and the one who wove the earth;
if the sky and the earth have come together,
why haven't we?

"Let's fetch water from the same well,
hunt in the same mountain,
eat by the same firepit,
and settle in the same shelter."

Zhemi Ma answered: "About this you must ask your father
and your mother.
Only when your father agrees can we get married,
and only when your mother agrees can we get married."

Zhepa Ma said: "I have no father
or mother,
so let's ask Heaven
to see if it is the will of Heaven."

Zhepa Ma pointed to the grinding stones and said:
"If I roll the grinding top from the East Mountain,
you roll the grinding bed from the West Mountain,
and the plates come together, let's get married."

Zhemi Ma pointed to the two mountains and said:
"If I burn the firewood in the North Mountain,
you burn the firewood in the South Mountain,
and the two mountain fires mix with their smoke, let's get
married."

遮帕麻上东山，
遮米麻上西山，
东山滚下磨盖，
西山滚下磨盘。

西山磨底滚到山脚，
东山磨盖滚到山底，
磨盖磨底心对心，
紧紧合在一起。

遮帕麻上南山，
遮米麻上北山，
两山同时点柴火，
两山同时冒火烟。

南山火烟向北，
北山火烟向南，
两山火烟相交，
合成一股青烟在高空盘旋。

山头火烟相交，
山底磨盘相合，
遮帕麻和遮米麻，
从此做了一家。

After Zhepa Ma went up the East Mountain,
and Zhemi Ma, the West Mountain,
the grinding top rolled down the East Mountain,
and the griding bed, the West Mountain.

As the grinding bed rolled to the foot of the West Mountain,
the grinding top rolled to the bottom of the East Mountain,
the top and bed coincided heart to heart,
tightly put together.

While Zhepa Ma got up the South Mountain,
Zhemi Ma, the North Mountain,
and then the fire started at the same time
and the smoke appeared at the same time.

The flame from the South Mountain heading north,
while the flame from the North Mountain going south,
the two flames from mountains intersected,
forming one blue puff hovering high in the sky.

After the intersection of the flames on the mountaintops
and the getting together of the grindstones at the mountain
bottom,
Zhepa Ma and Zhemi Ma
formed one family.

结婚九年才怀胎，
怀胎九年才临产，
生下一颗葫芦籽，
把它种在大门旁。

九年葫芦才发芽，
发芽九年才开花，
开花九年才结果，
结了一个葫芦有磨盘大。

遮帕麻走到葫芦下，
葫芦里面闹喳喳。
剖开葫芦看一看，
跳出九个小娃娃。

老大跳出来，
看见园里开桃花。
以"陶"（桃）为姓是汉族，
住到平坝种庄稼。

老二跳出来，
看见长刀挂在葫芦架。
以"刀"为姓是傣族，
住在河边捕鱼虾。

It took them nine years to conceive
and another nine years to give birth
to a gourd seed,
which they planted by the gate.

It took the seed nine years to sprout,
another nine years to flower,
and another nine years to yield the fruit
of a gourd as large as a millstone.

When Zhepa Ma walked under the gourd,
he heard the bustling sound inside.
When he cut it open to take a look,
nine little babies jumped out of it.

The eldest jumped out
and saw the peach tree blossoming in the garden.
Surnamed "Tao" (peach), he was of the Han Nationality
and lived on the flatland to grow crops.

The second jumped out
and saw the long knife hanging on the gourd trellis.
Surnamed "Dao" (knife), he was of the Dai Nationality
and lived near the river to catch fish and shrimp.

老三跳出来，
看见李树开白花。
以"李"为姓是白族，
洱海边上去安家。

老四跳出来，
听见门前河水响哗哗。
以"和"(河)为姓是纳西，
丽江坝子去养马。

老五跳出来，
看见牛打架。
以"牛"为姓是哈尼，
向阳山坡去种茶。

老六跳出来，
看见竹箩靠墙下。
以"罗"(箩)为姓是彝族，
彝族力大背盐巴。

老七跳出来，
看见石板光又滑。
以"石"为姓是景颇，
打把长刀肩上挎。

The third jumped out

and saw the plum tree with white flowers.

Surnamed "Li" (plum), he was of the Bai (white) Nationality

and settled near Lake Erhai.

The fourth jumped out

and heard the river in front of the door burbling.

Surnamed "He" (river), he was of the Naxi Nationality

and bred horses on the flatland of Lijiang.

The fifth jumped out

and saw the cows fighting.

Surnamed "Niu" (cow), he was of the Hani Nationality

and grow tea on the sunny mountain slope.

The sixth jumped out

and saw a bamboo basket leaning against the wall.

Surnamed "Luo" (basket), he was of the Yi Nationality

and carried salt with exceptional strength.

The seventh jumped out

and saw the stone slab smooth and shiny.

Surnamed "Shi" (stone), he was of the Jing Nationality

and smithed swords to be carried on the shoulder.

老八跳出来，
看见杨柳吐新芽。
以"杨"为姓是德昂，
德昂纺线弹棉花。

老九是个小姑娘，
遮米麻最喜欢她，
留在身边学织布，
织出腰带似彩霞。

老九很勤快，
天天起得早。
以"早"为姓是阿昌，
阿昌住在半山腰。

九种民族同是一个爹，
九种民族同是一个妈，
九种民族子孙多得像星星，
九种民族原本是一家。

The eighth jumped out
and saw the willows bursting of buds.
Surnamed "Liu" (willow), he was of the De'ang Nationality
and spun threads and loosened the cotton wool.

The ninth was a girl,
whom Zhemi Ma doted on
and kept around to learn weaving,
weaving waist belts like the rosy clouds.

The ninth was very diligent,
getting up early every day.
Surnamed "Zao" (early), he was of the Achang Nationality
and lived on the mountainside.

The nine nationalities had the same father
and the same mother.
The nine nationalities had grandchildren as many as the stars,
but they all are of the same family.

第二部分　补天治水

自古有阴就有阳，
自古有恶也有善，
有福便有祸，
祸福常相伴。

没有雨水鲜花不会开放，
雨水多了江河又会泛滥。
雨水给阿昌带来过幸福，
雨水也给阿昌制造过灾难。

阿昌的子孙啊，
要是窝铺漏雨，
不要责怪雨水，
赶快把房顶修理。

Chapter Two　Mending Heaven and Regulating Water

Since ancient times, where there is Yin, there is Yang,

and there is evil as well as good,

blessings followed by disasters,

the blessings and disasters that always accompanying each other.

Without the rainwater, flowers will not blossom,

but too much water causes rivers to flood.

Rain has brought happiness to Achang,

but also disasters to them.

Ah, the offspring of Achang,

if the roof leaks,

don't blame the rain,

but hurry and repair it.

第一折　遮米麻补天

阿昌、景颇住山寨，
山上有了砍柴打猎人；
汉族、傣家住平坝，
坝子有了种田打鱼人。

绿绿的庄稼长得好，
肥壮的牛羊跑满山。
风调雨顺的好日子啊，
过了七七四十九年。

不知哪年哪月的一个早晨，
东方的太阳还没有升起，
寨子里的人们还在安睡，
灾难忽然降临。

地下掀起狂风，
天上堆满黑云，
阳春三月下暴雨，
四十九天还不停。

高山被摧崩，
深谷被填满，
树林被扫平，
日月失去了光芒。

I . Zhemi Ma Mending the Sky

Achang and Jingpo lived in the villages in the mountains,

where now were woodcutters and hunters;

Han and Dai people lived on the flatland,

where now were farmers and fishermen.

As the green crops grew well,

the strong cattle and sheep ran all over the mountains.

Ah, the days of auspicious winds and rains,

lasted forty-nine years.

One morning of a certain year and month,

before the sunrise in the east,

when people in the village were still sleeping,

disaster befell.

With wild wind blowing on the earth,

and dark clouds covering the entire sky,

a rainstorm in the springly March

didn't stop for forty-nine days.

The rain destroyed the mountains,

filled up the deep valleys,

swept away the woodland,

and the sun and the moon lost their shine.

春天的雷雨，
把窝里的小鸟打落；
铺天盖地的洪水，
淹没了山寨村落。

大地变成了一片汪洋，
山峰像一只漂荡的小船。
白天看不见太阳，
晚上看不见月亮。

不是遮帕麻造小了天，
也不是遮米麻抽地筋。
是天地没有合拢，
狂风卷起了天的四边。

天破了地母会补，
她早已把三根地筋绕成了线团。
三根地筋用来补天，
缝合了天地的三个边缘。

第一根地筋缝合了东边的天地，
太阳和月亮从那儿升起。
东边不再刮大风，
东边不再下暴雨。

The thunderstorm in the spring
knocked off the chicks in the nests;
the overwhelming flood
drowned all mountain villages.

The earth became an ocean,
and the mountain peak was like a drifting small boat.
The sun was not seen during the day,
nor was the moon seen at night.

It was not because Zhepa Ma made the sky too small,
or Zhemi Ma pulled the tendons of the earth.
It was because the sky and the earth did not close tightly
enough
and so the wind rolled up the four sides of the sky.

The earth goddess knew how to mend the broken sky,
having made the three earth's tendons into a ball of yarn.
The three earth's tendons were used to mend the sky,
mending three sides of it.

The first tendon was used to attach the sky and earth in the
east,
where the sun and the moon rose up.
The strong gale stopped in the east,
so did the heavy rainstorm.

第二根地筋缝合了西边的天地，
太阳和月亮到那儿歇息。
西边不再刮大风，
西边不再下暴雨。

第三根地筋缝合了北边的天地，
北斗高挂笑眯眯。
北边不再刮冷风，
北边不再下暴雨。

缝好东、西、北三边天地，
三根地筋已经用尽。
南边的天地无线补，
南边的暴雨还在下个不停。

The second tendon was used to attach the sky and earth in
the west,
　　where the sun and the moon set.
　　The strong gales stopped in the west,
　　so did the heavy rainstorm.

The third tendon was used to attach the sky and earth in the
north,
　　where the smiling Big Dipper hung.
　　The cold wind stopped in the north,
　　so did the heavy rainstorm.

Mending the east, west, and north sides of the sky and
earth
　　took all three tendons.
　　With no tendon to attach the sky and earth in the south,
　　the rainstorm continued there.

第二折　遮帕麻造南天门

要补南边的天，
要救南方的难，
天公告别地母，
去到南方拉涅旦。

高山挡住去路，
遮帕麻挥动赶山鞭，
群山像驯服的牛羊，
听从遮帕麻驱赶。

河水挡住去路，
遮帕麻横放赶山鞭，
鞭子变成一座桥，
跨到了河的对岸。

遮帕麻来到拉涅旦，
这里还是一片汪洋。
没有地线缝补南天，
只好筑一道遮风挡雨的墙。

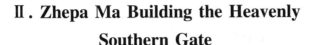

II. Zhepa Ma Building the Heavenly Southern Gate

To mend the sky in the south,
to rescue the south,
the heaven god left the earth goddess,
and went to Laniedan in the south.

When the high mountains blocked the path,
Zhepa Ma waved his mountain-driving whip,
and the mountains were like tamed cattle and sheep
heeding Zhepa Ma's orders.

When the river blocked the path,
Zhepa Ma lay his mountain-driving whip down,
so that the whip became a bridge
to help him cross the river.

Zhepa Ma reached Laniedan,
where he found what was still an ocean.
With no earth thread to mend the sky in the south,
he had to build a wall to keep out the wind and the rain.

筑墙要用九拿长的石头，
修门要用九丈宽的木板。
找石头要到九十九里外，
找木板九十九天才回转。

神兵抬石脚打战，
神将解板汗如雨。
做重活啊太劳倦，
一个个浑身无力摇摇晃晃。

拉涅旦有个智慧的盐婆，
名字叫作桑姑尼。
她炒菜放盐巴，
将士吃了才又有了力气。

木板做框石垒墙，
筑起南天门来挡风雨。
南方不再刮大风，
南天不再下暴雨。

拉涅旦的天空又出现了彩霞，
拉涅旦的大地又种上了庄稼。
风刮断了的大树重发新枝，
水泡烂了的藤子又吐新芽。

He needed nine hands long stones to construct the wall

and nine *zhang* broad boards to build the frame.

He had to walk ninety-nine *li* to find the stones

and spend ninety-nine days to find the boards.

Lifting the stones, the heavenly soldiers' feet trembled,

and unloading the boards, the heavenly generals' sweat poured.

The demanding work took its toll,

and they all felt weak and could hardly walk steadily.

In Laniedan there was a wise salt lady

Sangguni.

She cooked with salt,

which helped the generals and soldiers regain their strength.

With the wooden boards as the frame and the stones as the wall,

the Heavenly Southern Gate was built to block the wind and rain.

There was no more wild winds blowing

or heavy rains destroying.

Laniedan saw that the rosy clouds reappeared in the sky

and crops were replanted on the earth.

The big trees broken by the wind rebranched,

and the vines rotten by the floodwater resprouted.

枯树发芽靠春风，
拉涅旦离不开恩人遮帕麻。
青藤喜缠大青树，
桑姑尼爱上了英雄遮帕麻。

Resprouting of the withered tree depends on the spring breeze,

and Laniedan was eternally indebted to Zhepa Ma.

As green vines happily winding up the big green trees,

Sangguni fell in love with hero Zhepa Ma.

第三部分　妖魔乱世

阿昌的子孙啊，
风不刮树树不弯，
水蛇不撵鱼，
池塘不会起波浪。

豹子出了窝，
黄麂子就要满山逃窜。
世上有了妖魔，
百姓就要遭受苦难。

正当鲜花开得最香，
正当稻谷熟得最黄，
正当牛羊长得最壮，
大地中央却出了个乱世魔王。

Chapter Three   The Demon Attempting to Ruin the World

Ah, the offspring of Achang,

just as without the wind, trees do not bend,

without water snakes chasing the fish,

the pond does not have waves.

Once the leopard comes out of the den,

the yellow muntjacs flee all over the mountain.

Once demons appear in the world,

common people suffer hardships.

Just when the flowers bloomed with its best fragrance,

the rice ripened at its most yellow,

the cattle and sheep grew at their strongest,

a demon king showed up in the center of the earth.

第一折　腊訇作乱

世界像一只手掌，
故事发生在手掌的中央。
遮米麻在家织布，
遮帕麻还在南方。

妖精腊訇出世了，
他是一个凶狠的魔王。
但不知他生在哪里，
也不知他来自何方。

腊訇有兵有将，
心毒手辣像恶狼：
刚刚来到大地中央，
便想独霸这块地方。

他翻着眼睛看太阳，
心里在恶毒地盘算：
遮帕麻造的太阳，
升起还要降。

世上发光发亮的东西，
都是热乎乎的一团；
遮帕麻造的月亮，
有光无热空挂天上。

I. Lahong Making Trouble

If the world were a palm,

then the story had taken place in the center of the palm.

Zhemi Ma was weaving at home,

while Zhepa Ma was still in the south.

Demon Lahong was born,

a fierce demon king to be.

No one knows where he was born,

where he came from.

With soldiers and generals,

Lahong was as cruel as a wolf:

As soon as he came to the center of the earth,

he wanted to dominate it.

Turning his eyes towards the sun,

he made a vicious plan:

The sun made by Zhepa Ma

rose but also set.

The glowing things in the world

were all warm;

the moon made by Zhepa Ma

hung with light but no warmth in the sky.

我要造一个不会落的太阳，
让世界只有白天没有夜晚，
让人们不分昼夜做活路，
让我的名声永远传扬。

腊訇使尽牛力气，
射上去一个假太阳，
牢牢钉在天幕上，
不会升也不会降。

遮米麻在家织布纺线，
手也麻了，脚也酸了，
织出的布已有九丈长，
怎么天空还是亮堂堂？

走出门来看一看，
太阳高高挂天上。
不知它何时才落山呀，
心里好生奇怪。

她等着太阳落，
可是等了三年还不降。
天空好像燃烈火，
地面比烧红的锅还烫。

I will make a sun that will never set,

making the world have no night but day,

causing people to work day and night,

and spreading my reputation forever.

With all his strength,

Lahong shoot up a fake sun

and nailed it on the sky tightly,

a sun that knew no rising or setting.

Zhemi Ma was weaving at home,

her hands numb and feet sour,

the woven cloth nine *zhang* long,

but why was the sun still bright in the sky?

Going out to look,

she saw the sun still hanging high.

Oh! When will the sun set,

she wondered anxiously.

She waited for three years for the sun to set,

but it did not.

The sky was like the burning fire,

and the earth was hotter than a broiled pot.

水塘烤干了，
树林晒枯了，
土地开裂了，
再没有地方躲阴凉了。

水牛的角晒弯了，
从此水牛的角是弯的了；
黄牛的皮烤黄了，
从此黄牛的皮是黄的了。

野猪的背脊烧煳了，
从此野猪脊背是黑的了；
猫头鹰被晒怕了，
从此猫头鹰在白天闭着眼睛了。

鸭子把嗓子哭哑了，
从此鸭子是哑嗓；
飞蝉把肠子气断了，
从此飞蝉没有了肚肠。

腊訇颠倒了阴阳，
整个世界一片混乱：
山族动物被赶下水，
水族动物被赶上山。

With the pond sun-grilled,

the woods sun-scorched

and the land sun-cracked,

there was not a place of shade.

The horn of the buffalo was sun-bent,

the way its horn has been curved ever since;

the skin of the cattle was sun-roasted yellow,

the color the yellow cattle has had ever since.

The back of the wild boar was burned,

the black back the wild boar has had ever since;

the owl was sun-scared,

the way the owl shuts its eyes during the day ever since.

The duck cried its voice hoarse,

the hoarse voice the duck has had ever since;

the cicada broke its intestines with anger,

the intestines it has not had ever since.

Lahong violated the Yin and Yang,

causing chaos to the whole world:

Mountain animals were driven into the waters,

while aquariums were forced up the mountains.

树木倒着生，
竹根朝天长，
游鱼在山头打滚，
走兽在水里漂荡。

一条大鱼滚到山凹里，
硬着头皮朝土里钻，
鱼鳞烤硬变甲壳，
鱼头烤焦了缩成一团。

这条大鱼变成了穿山甲，
打个山洞躲太阳，
钻在里边不露影，
捕捉蚂蚁做食粮。

蛇毒毒不过七步青，
心狠狠不过腊訇精。
世界沉入火海里，
腊訇更加得意忘形：

"遮帕麻造的天再大，
没有我的神通大；
遮米麻织的地再宽，
不够我把魔法施展。

Trees grew upside down,
and bamboo roots grew towards the sky,
the fish rolled on the hilltops,
and the beasts drifted in the water.

A large fish rolled into the mountain pit,
dove persistently its head into the soil,
sun-grilled its scales hard into a shell,
and sun-burnt its head into a wrinkled-up ball.

This big fish became the pangolin,
who digs caves to hide from the sun,
hides inside without showing its face,
and captures ants for food.

Just as no snake is more poisonous than the sharp-nosed pit
viper,
no one is more cruel than Demon Lahong.
The more the world sank into the sea of fire,
the happier Lahong was beyond himself:

"No matter how large Zhepa Ma made the sky,
it is no larger than the power of my magic;
no matter how broad Zhemi Ma built the earth,
it is no broader than the reach of my magic.

"天上地下我都要管，
强者就要做大王。
谁敢阻拦我，
叫他活不长。

"杀谁留谁全在我，
不管别人怎么说，
东西南北我安排，
生生死死我掌握。"

被恶狼冲散的羊群，
会咩咩地把主人叫唤；
被狂风吹散的小鸟，
会啾啾地寻找伙伴。

看到生灵遭到灾难，
遮米麻心急似油煎。
无力制伏腊訇啊，
她日日夜夜盼着遮帕麻回还。

"I will oversee all in the sky and on the earth,

because the strong must be the king.

Whoever dares to stop me,

I won't let them live long.

I decide who dies and who lives,

no matter what others say,

decide where the east, west, south and north are,

and decide everything pertains to life or death."

The flocks scattered by the evil wolf

will bleat for their owner;

the birds scattered by the violent wind

will chirp to find their partners.

Seeing all lives were suffering the disaster,

Zhemi Ma was burning with anxiety.

Ah, unable to subdue Lahong,

she was looking forward day and night to Zhepa Ma's

return.

第二折　水獭猫送信

遮帕麻南行的时候，
曾站在家门口，
指着南流的河水对遮米麻说：
"我就顺着这条河走。

"南边的天补好了，
我就叫河水倒着流，
让它回来报信，
你在家里把我等候。"

想起遮帕麻的留言，
遮米麻天天去到河边：
看滔滔的流水啊，
有没有倒流回来。

早上跑三转，
下午跑三转，
晚上跑三转，
一天跑九转。

望着南去的流水，
遮米麻大声呼唤：
"清清的流水呀，
快快流到拉涅旦。

II. The Otter Sending Massage

Before Zhepa Ma left for the south,

he once stood at the gate,

and pointing to the river running south, said to Zhemi Ma:

"I will go along this river.

"When the sky in the south was mended,

I will let the river flow backward

to let it send the message to you,

so just wait for me at home."

With what Zhepa Ma had said in mind,

Zhemi Ma went to the river every day:

Ah, the flowing water,

had it flowed backward yet?

Going to the river three times in the morning,

three times in the afternoon,

three times in the evening,

she went nine times a day.

Looking at the flowing water towards the south,

Zhemi Ma shouted:

"Ah, clear water,

quickly flow to Laniedan.

"请带个信给遮帕麻，
就说生灵遭祸殃，
魔王霸占了天地，
叫他赶快把家还。"

看着滚滚南流水，
总是不见它折头。
遮米麻两眼都望穿，
心里又添一层愁。

向着南边的天，
遮米麻大声地呼唤：
"遮帕麻啊遮帕麻，
你要快快把家还。"

南边的天空空荡荡，
听不到一声回响。
南天上的云彩停下了脚步，
信儿怎么传得到南方？

忽然看见两只狗，
正在河里游，
遮米麻立刻跑上去，
站在河边请求：

"Please bring a message to Zhepa Ma,
that all lives are suffering the disaster
of a demon king who seized the heaven and earth,
and let him return home quickly."

Looking at the roaring water running south,
she never saw the water running backward.
Zhemi Ma almost strained her eyes blind,
but all she got was another layer of worry.

To the south
Zhemi Ma shouted:
"Oh, Zhepa Ma, Zhepa Ma,
return home quickly."

From the empty south sky,
she heard no reply.
Even the clouds in the southern sky paused,
so how to send the message to the south?

Suddenly she saw two dogs
swimming in the river,
so she ran up quickly
and pleaded with them from the bank of the river:

"小狗啊小狗，
赶快顺水游，
踩着遮帕麻的脚印走，
叫他回来把妖魔收。"

两只小狗摇摇头：
"拉涅旦山高路难走，
从头到尾几千里，
不知要跑到什么时候！

"腊旬把我们赶下水，
空长四脚不能走。
叫我送信我高兴，
要游几千里怎能忍受！

"路上饿了没吃的，
碰上老虎要丢命。
遮米麻啊，我们实在害怕，
还是让我们留在这里。"

听了狗的话，
遮米麻急得直搓手：
信儿送不到，
妖魔怎么收？

"Oh, little puppy, little puppy,

swim downstream quickly,

following Zhepa Ma's footprints,

and tell him to come back to defeat the demon."

The two puppies shook their heads:

"Laniedan being far and high,

a total of several thousands of *li* from here to there,

who knows how long we will have to run!

"After Lahong drove us down the water,

we can't walk with our four legs.

I would be happy to send the message,

but could not endure thousands of *li* of swimming!

"We will have no food to eat when hungry,

and lose our lives when encountering the tiger.

Ah, Zhemi Ma, we are really scared,

so please let us stay here."

After listening to the dogs,

Zhemi Ma was so anxious with her hands wringing:

If the message was undeliverable,

how would the demon be defeated?

忽然又见两只鸡，
漂在河里顺水流，
遮米麻赶快跑上去，
站在河边请求：

"小鸡啊小鸡，
赶快往南游，
踩着遮帕麻的脚印走，
叫他回来把妖魔收。"

小鸡摇头开口讲：
"太阳我能叫出山，
但远在南边的遮帕麻呀，
我无法把他叫回来。

"腊訇把我赶下水，
不许上岸回窝里。
派我送信我高兴，
可惜我打湿了的翅膀不会飞。

"路上饿了没吃的，
碰上野猫更倒霉。
遮米麻啊，我们实在没本领，
还是让我们留在这里。"

Suddenly she saw two chickens

drifting with the river,

so Zhemi Ma ran up hurriedly

and pleaded with them from the bank of the river:

"Ah, little chicken, little chicken,

swim quickly to the south,

follow Zhepa Ma's footprints,

and tell him to come back and defeat the demon."

The two chickens shook their heads:

"We can call the sun to rise,

but Zhepa Ma who is in the far south

we cannot call back.

"Ever since Lahong drove us down the river,

we can't go ashore to return to our nests.

We would be happy to send the message,

but it's a pity that we cannot fly with the wet wings.

"We have no food to eat when hungry on the road

and will be even more unlucky when encountering the wild

cats.

Ah, Zhemi Ma, we are really unable to help,

so please let us stay here."

听了小鸡的话，
遮米麻急得流眼泪：
信儿送不到，
遮帕麻何时才得归？

有只水獭猫，
自自在在漂水上：
调水它比鱼灵活，
上岸跑得比狗快。

腊匐把它撺下水，
吃鱼吃虾饿不倒；
腊匐把它赶上山，
打个山洞能安家。

它看见遮米麻啊，
坐在岸边淌眼泪，
便张开笑脸走上来，
说几句宽心话来安慰：

"遮米麻啊好奶奶，
什么事情想不开？
有了难处告诉我，
有什么事情我来帮忙。"

After listening to the chicken,

Zhemi Ma was more anxious with tears running:

If the message was undeliverable,

when would Zhepa Ma be back?

There was an otter,

drifting on the water at ease:

It swam more dexterously than the fish

and ran faster than the dog on the shore.

Lahong drove him down the water,

but he caught fish and shrimp to eat with no hunger.

Lahong drove him up the mountain,

but he dug a cave and settled down.

Seeing Zhemi Ma

who sat on the shore in tears,

the otter walked up to her with a smile

and offered some reassuring words:

"Oh, Zhemi Ma, good grandma,

what's the problem?

Tell me about it,

and I will give you a hand."

遮米麻听了多欢喜，
抱起水獭猫把泪揩净。
指着太阳骂腊旬，
望着南方直叹气：

"你看这天不像天，
你看这地不像地，
世界成了这个样，
叫我怎么不着急！

"只有叫回遮帕麻，
才能除掉魔王。
信要送到拉涅旦，
只好派你前往。

"水獭猫你听仔细，
我的嘱托莫忘记：
跑在山上别贪玩，
游在水里莫大意。

"顺着遮帕麻的脚印走，
快快赶到拉涅旦去，
喊回天公，重整天地，
那时我招你做女婿。"

水獭猫点点头：
"奶奶不用愁，
信儿我去送，
不见到天公不折头！"

How happy Zhemi Ma was when she heard these words,
so she picked up the otter and wiped away her tears.
Pointing to the sun, scolding Lahong,
and looking to the south, she sighed:

"The sky not being the sky,
the earth not being the earth,
the world having become like this,
how could I not worry!

"Only if Zhepa Ma is called back,
can the demon be rid of.
The message must be sent to Laniedan,
and you are the only one who can do it.

"Ah, Otter, listen carefully
to keep my message in mind:
Don't be distracted when running on the mountain
or careless while swimming in the water.

"If you follow Zhepa Ma's footprints,
get to Laniedan as soon as possible,
call back the god of the sky to restore the world,
I will take you as my son-in-law."

The otter nodded:
"Don't worry, granny.
I will send the message,
and I will not return until I see the heaven god!"

这只可爱的水獭猫，
不怕水深山高，
朝着遥远的拉涅旦，
睁大眼睛拼命跑。

翻了九十九座山，
过了九十九条河。
肚子空了不知饿，
嗓子干了不知渴。

这只机灵的水獭猫，
不知跑了多少路程。
肉跑掉了九斤，
皮磨破了九层。

身上的毛结成了疙瘩，
头上沾满了灰尘，
嗓子干得说不出话，
肚子饿得头发昏。

忽然看到一片椰子林，
林中有个小村庄。
村外一眼井，
井水清汪汪。

水獭猫想进村，
去把遮帕麻打听。
可身上脏得不像样，
邋里邋遢不好见人。

This lovely otter,

fearless of the deep waters and high mountains,

towards the remote Laniedan,

ran as fast as it could with its eyes wide open.

The otter went over ninety-nine mountains

and crossed ninety-nine rivers.

It knew no hunger though its stomach was empty

or thirst though its throat was dry.

This clever otter

ran countless miles.

It lost weight of nine *jin*

and worn out nine layers of its skin.

The hair on its body in knots,

its head covered in dust,

its throat too dry to speak,

the otter became dizzy with hunger.

Finally, he came across a coconut forest,

where there was a small village.

Outside the village was a well,

its water bright and clear.

The otter wanted to go into the village

to ask about Zhepa Ma.

But he was too filthy,

and too messy to see people.

看着清汪汪的水，
水獭猫纵身跳下井。
先喝水，后洗澡，
又是翻身又打滚。

干渴全解了，
皮毛洗亮了，
身上凉快了，
却把井水搅浑了。

水獭猫跳到草地上，
放平身子烤太阳。
一路奔跑太劳累，
躺在地上睡得香。

寨门吱呀响，
走出一个挑水的女人：
上坡好像柳迎风，
下坡好像风送云。

她的头发比燕子毛还黑，
她的脸比鹭鸶毛还白，
她牙齿比石榴籽还密，
这个美人就是桑姑尼。

The otter saw the clear water

and jumped into the well.

It drank the water and bathed itself,

turning over and rolling about.

It drank its heart's content,

washed its fur shiny,

cooled itself all over,

but muddied the well water.

The otter jumped onto the grass,

laid itself flat to sunbathe.

He was so exhausted from running all the way

that he slept a sound sleep.

With the creaking of the village gate,

a woman came out to fetch water:

She looked like the willow greeting the wind when walking

uphill

and the cloud sending off the wind when walking downhill.

With hair darker than the swallow fur,

a face whiter than the egret hair,

and teeth denser than the pomegranate seeds,

this beauty was Sangguni.

她来到井边，
刚刚打起一桶水来，
就吓了一大跳：
清清的井水变成了泥浆！

阿公阿祖留下话，
井水变浑地要塌。
桑姑尼水也不敢挑，
急急忙忙转回家。

忽然看见水獭猫，
呼呼大睡正打鼾。
定下心来仔细看，
水獭猫身上的水汽还不干。

桑姑尼心里直冒火，
张开嘴巴大声骂：
"哪里来的野东西！"
提起扁担就要打。

水獭猫惊醒了，
一骨碌跳起来，
躲开桑姑尼的扁担，
边说话边揉眼：

She came to the well,

pulled up a bucket of water,

and then was startled:

The clear water had turned into mud!

Grandpa and Grandma had said,

muddy well water meant the ground would collapse.

Sangguni did not dare to continue with fetching the water

and hurried back home.

Then she saw the otter,

snoring loudly in its sleep.

She calmed herself down, took a closer look,

and found the water on the otter was still not dried up.

Sangguni was filled with anger

and stared to scold the otter loudly:

"Where came this wild thing!"

She picked up the shoulder pole and was about to hit it.

The otter woke up with a start,

jumped up with one roll of its body,

escaped Sangguni's shoulder pole,

and said while rubbing its eyes:

"我是北方来的客呀，
遮米麻派我来找遮帕麻。
妖魔腊訇作乱了，
这音信要当面告诉他。"

听说来找遮帕麻，
桑姑尼的眼睛亮了，
桑姑尼的心里乐了，
高高举起的扁担放下了。

"遮帕麻就住在我家，
跟着我就能见到他。
今天他去打麂子，
太阳落山才回家。

"你是北方来的客，
我回家给你泡茶。
肚子饿了不用愁，
我家里有鱼也有虾。"

水獭猫心里欢喜，
跟着盐婆就走。
刚要跨进门，
一跳跳到桑姑尼的肩头：

"Hey, I am the guest from the north,
sent by Zhemi Ma to find Zhepa Ma.
Demon Lahong has caused chaos,
which is the message I must give him in person."

Hearing that he came to find Zhepa Ma,
Sangguni's eyes lit up,
and she was filled with joy,
so she put down her raised pole.

"Zhepa Ma lives in my house,
so follow me and you'll see him.
Today he has gone to hunt muntjacs
and will be back when the sun sets.

"Since you are a guest from the north,
I'll go home and make some tea for you.
Don't worry if you are hungry,
because I have fish and shrimp."

The otter was delighted
and followed the Lady Salt to her home.
When they were about to step into the gate,
the otter jumped onto Sangguni's shoulder:

"奶奶奶奶我害怕，
我的身上有股怪味道，
你家的猎狗恶，
闻到骚味会把我咬。"

"水獭猫，你别害怕，
猎狗撵山不在家。
回头你就躲在屋梁上，
等我栓好猎狗再下来。"

遮帕麻打猎一整天，
麂子的影子都不见，
辛辛苦苦无收获，
两手空空下山来。

半路碰上瓢泼大雨，
从头到脚都淋遍，
泥浆溅在身上，
愁苦挂在脸上。

到家赶走了兵和将，
烧起火塘烤衣裳。
湿柴点火火不燃，
不见火苗只冒烟。

黑烟腾腾冲屋梁，
熏坏了梁上的水獭猫：
又是咳嗽又流泪，
一边叫喊一边跳。

"Grandma, grandma, I'm afraid
because my body has a strange smell
that your vicious hunting dog can detect
and will attack me."

"Otter, don't be afraid!
The hunting dog has been out running in the mountains.
When it comes back later, you hide among the roof beams
and come down after I have tied it up."

Though Zhepa Ma had hunted for a whole day,
he hadn't seen the shadow of a muntjac.
Without harvest from his hard work,
he came down the mountain empty-handed.

Half way through his returning trip the rain poured,
drenching him from head to toe,
splashing mud on his body,
putting sorrow on his face.

When he arrived home, he let go the soldiers and generals,
lit the firepit to dry his clothes.
The wet firewood would not start the fire,
so no flame but only the smoke was seen.

When the black smoke rose to the roof beams,
the otter on the beam suffered greatly:
Coughing and crying,
he shouted and jumped at the same time.

遮帕麻看见水獭猫，
抓起棒棒就要打：
"满山找不着一根鹿子毛，
想不到野物自己送到家！"

吼声传进厨房里，
急坏了正在做饭的桑姑尼：
"快住手，别动气，
它是北边来的小东西。"

听说水獭猫从家乡来，
遮帕麻的怒气顿时消。
连忙抱下小东西，
一面问好一面笑。

水獭猫跳上遮帕麻的肩膀，
咬着耳朵把音信传：
"腊訇乱世搅窝子，
遮米麻盼你快回还……"

阿昌族、德昂族古典史诗 Classical Epics of Achang and De'ang

Zhepa Ma saw the otter

and grabbed the stick about to hit it:

"Not a single muntjac hair was found all over the mountain,

but who knew a wild animal has presented itself to me at

home!"

When the roar was heard in the kitchen,

Sangguni who was cooking was alarmed:

"Please stop quickly and don't get angry

at this little thing who came from the north."

Hearing that the otter came from his hometown,

Zhepa Ma immediately calmed down.

Hurriedly picking up the little thing,

he said hello and smiled at the same time.

The moment the otter jumped onto Zhepa Ma's shoulder,

into his ear he said the message:

"Lahong has made trouble in the world,

and Zhemi Ma wants you to go home as soon as possible..."

第三折　遮帕麻回归

激怒了的大象，
会把竹林踏平。
惊人的消息啊，
撕碎了遮帕麻的心：

"一拃长的花蛇，
竟想吞下大象！
故乡的百姓正在遭殃，
我怎能不去救难！"

遮帕麻收拾行装要上路，
桑姑尼心里乱如麻。
她走上前来拉着他，
眼里泪水如雨下：

"遮帕麻啊遮帕麻，
拉涅旦哺育我长大，
要我离开这里哟，
心里实在放不下。

"离开抱我长大的阿爹，
离开养我长大的阿妈，
离开我朝夕相处的兄妹，
我的心啊似刀剐。

III. Zhepa Ma Returning Home

An enraged elephant
could flatten a bamboo forest.
The alarming news
tore apart the heart of Zhepa Ma：

"A span long poisonous snake
wants to swallow an elephant!
The people in my hometown are suffering,
so I must go to rescue them!"

As Zhepa Ma was packing for the trip,
Sangguni's heart was in turmoil.
She walked up and touched him,
with tears running down like the rain：

"Zhepa Ma, ah, Zhepa Ma,
Laniedan has nurtured me,
so to leave here
I really cannot.

"Leaving my dad who has held me
and my mom who has raised me,
and my siblings with whom I have spent my days,
I am heart-broken.

"砍下我的两腿留在家吧，
免得爹妈和兄妹常牵挂！
可是归途九千里，
没有腿怎么把山爬！

"砍下我的双手留在家吧，
免得爹妈和兄妹常牵挂！
可是路程九千里，
没有手怎么抱娃娃！

"砍下我的脑壳留在家吧，
免得爹妈和兄妹常牵挂！
可是没有脑壳不能活哟，
怎能跟你回去熬盐巴！

"双腿不能不留着，
双手不能不留着，
脑壳不能不留着，
遮帕麻啊还是留下吧！"

听说遮帕麻要回家，
拉涅旦的百姓也苦苦留他：
"遮帕麻啊你不能走，
这里就是你的家。

阿昌族、德昂族古典史诗 Classical Epics of Achang and De'ang

104

"I could cut off my legs and leave them at home,
so that my parents and siblings won't worry about me!
But it is nine thousand *li* away,
so how can I climb the mountain without the legs!

"I could cut off my arms and leave them at home,
so that my parents and siblings won't worry about me!
But it is nine thousand *li* away,
so how can I carry the baby without the arms!

"I could cut off my head and leave it at home,
so that my parents and siblings won't worry about me!
But without a head, I cannot be alive,
so how can I go back with you to make salt!

"I cannot leave behind my legs,
my hands,
my head,
so, Zhepa Ma, please stay!"

On hearing that Zhepa Ma was going home,
the people of Laniedan also begged him to stay:
"Zhepa Ma, you can't leave here,
your home.

"我们离开了你，
就会像冬天的树桠；
我们离开了你，
就会像没有露珠的小草。"

十人围不过的大榕树，
狂风也不能把它摇动。
百姓的眼泪哟，
却使遮帕麻感动：

"你们诚心挽留，
我万分感激；
你们对我的爱戴，
我永远铭记。

"我跟北方、南方的百姓，
都心连着心；
是去还是留，
看天意来定。

"现在就派兵将去狩猎，
不打老虎也不打狐狸，
专撵山老鼠，
看它的行踪测天意。

"When we leave you,

we will be like the branches of winter trees;

when we leave you,

we will be like the grass without dewdrops."

The big banyan tree thicker than what ten people could hold

cannot be shaken by the strong wind.

But the tears of the people

moved Zhepa Ma:

"You sincerely want me to stay,

for which I am extremely grateful;

the love you have shown to me

I will remember forever."

"I and people in both the north and the south

are connected by hearts,

so whether I am going or staying

let Heaven decide.

"Now, I am sending troops to hunt,

hunting not tigers, not foxes,

but only the mountain mice,

whose moves can be examined to find the fate.

"老鼠出新洞、进旧洞，
天意要我回北方除魔王；
老鼠出旧洞、进新洞，
天意要我留在南方。"

兵将打猎回家来，
欢欢喜喜地讲：
"老鼠出新洞、进旧洞，
天意要你去除魔王。"

遮帕麻提起赶山鞭，
点齐兵将就要启程。
拉涅旦的百姓拦路哭，
离别的泪水湿透了衣襟：

"要高飞的金孔雀啊，
不要忘记你栖息过的地方；
要离开我们的遮帕麻啊，
不要忘记你居住过的村庄。"

"If the mouse goes out of a new hole and into an old one,

it means I am meant to return to the north to eliminate the

demon;

if the mouse comes out of an old hole and into a new one,

it means I should stay in the south."

When soldiers came home from hunting,

they spoke joyfully:

"The mouse went out of a new hole and into an old one,

so it is the will of Heaven that you go to eliminate the

demon."

Zhepa Ma picked up the mountain-driving whip,

organizing the troops for departure.

The people of Laniedan stood along the way and cried,

tears of parting soaking the front of their clothes:

"The gold peacock that wants to fly high,

do not forget the place where you rested;

Zhepa Ma who is about to leave us,

do not forget the village where you lived."

第四部分　降妖除魔

大山压顶的时候，
要挺直腰杆；
大难临头的时候，
要咬紧牙关。

天最黑的时候，
千万不要慌张：
黑暗总有尽头，
东方就要升起太阳。

Chapter Four　Subduing the Demon

When the mountain presses down again the head,
keep your back straight;
in times of impending disaster,
clench your teeth.

In the darkest of the night,
do not panic:
Darkness always has an end,
and the sun is about to rise in the east.

第一折　斗法

腊訇乱世三年，
大地闹了四年饥荒。
天底下没有一丝阴凉哟，
连大青树也都枯黄。

活着的百姓逃亡他乡，
死了的百姓堆满路旁。
专吃腐肉的乌鸦啊，
也伤心得眼泪汪汪。

天空飘过朵朵白云，
传来了下雨的消息；
聪明伶俐的水懒猫哟，
带来了遮帕麻回归的音信。

遮帕麻回到故乡，
遮米麻到山脚迎接。
不等天公进家门，
便滔滔倾诉心中的苦和恨：

"你看天上挂着一个假太阳，
使这里只有白天没有夜晚，
绿苗被烧焦，池水成泥塘，
魔王造下的罪孽说不完。

I. Competition of Mental Powers

During the three turbulent years of Lahong,
the earth suffered four years of famine.
Without a trace of shade in the world,
even the big green trees had withered and turned yellow.

Those who survived fled to other lands,
and those who died piled up along the roadside.
Ah, even the scavenger crows who ate only carrion
were sad with teary eyes.

Pieces of the white clouds floating across the sky
bring the news of the rain;
Ah, the smart and quick otter
brought the news of Zhepa Ma's return.

When Zhepa Ma returned to his hometown,
Zhemi Ma went to greet him at the foot of the mountain.
Before the Heaven God entered the house,
she poured out the bitterness and hatred in her heart:

"Look at the fake sun hanging in the sky,
which has caused this place to have only days and no
nights,
the seedlings to burn, the pond to become mud,
the sins of the demon king never end.

113

"腊訇这个大妖魔,
有兵有将会神通,
蝎子毒蛇没有他毒,
豺狼虎豹没有他凶。"

遮帕麻心里怒火烧,
一跳九丈高:
"妖精腊訇实在可恶,
不把他杀掉恨难消!"

遮帕麻挥起赶山鞭,
鞭响似雷炸。
他要马上和魔王打仗,
召来了所有的兵马。

可又转念一想:
"两只老虎打架,
会揉伤田里的禾苗,
不能让战争把百姓糟蹋。"

举起的赶山鞭又轻轻放下,
集合的兵马又解散回家:
"在腊訇喝水的河里撒毒药,
那才是一个好办法。"

"Lahong, this demon
has soldiers and generals with heavenly powers,
more poisonous than scorpions and venomous snakes,
fiercer than jackals, wolves, tigers, and leopards."

Zhepa Ma, with a burning anger in his heart,
jumped nine *zhang* high:
"Lahong Demon is too hateful,
the hatred that can only be rid of when he is eliminated!"

Zhepa Ma swung his mountain-driving whip,
which sounded like thunders cracking.
He wanted to fight the demon immediately
and summoned all the soldiers and horses.

But he thought again:
"Two tigers fighting
will damage the seedlings in the field,
but the war should not hurt the people."

The raised mountain-driving whip was put down gently,
and the assembled troops and horses were sent away:
"To poison the river where Lahong drinks water
is a good way."

遮米麻一听连忙制止：
"遮帕麻啊你想的不妥当。
没有水，生灵怎么生活？
毒药不能撒水上。"

遮帕麻想了想说：
"不撒水里撒山上。
野果山菜都沾着毒，
腊訇吃了烂肝肠。"

遮米麻又劝告：
"山上动物万万千，
即使把妖魔毒死了，
无辜生灵也要受牵连。"

遮帕麻急得团团转：
"那还有什么好主张？"
遮米麻早有主意在心头：
"莫着急，先去跟腊訇交朋友。

"交了朋友再斗法，
瞅准时机好下手。
再烈的火也克不过水，
作乱的妖魔定能收。"

Hearing it, Zhemi Ma put a stop to it quickly:
"Ah, Zhepa Ma, you are not thinking right.
How does the life survive without water?
You cannot put poison into the water."

Having thought about it more, Zhepa Ma said:
"If not the water, then the mountains can be the place.
If the wild berries and mountain vegetables are all poisonous,
Lahong will be killed by poison."

Again, Zhemi Ma advised:
"With countless animals in the mountains,
even if the demon is poisoned to death,
innocent lives will also be affected."

Zhepa Ma was anxious, pacing in circles:
"Is there any good idea then?"
Zhemi Ma already had an idea in her mind:
"Not to worry, and go and make friends with Lahong first.

"Making friends before fighting,
you can seize the opportunity to take action.
No matter how strong the fire is, it cannot withstand water,
so the disrupting demon will definitely be subdued."

遮帕麻来到腊訇家，
魔王翻翻白眼不说话，
一副鬼相，满脸怒气，
不让坐也不倒茶。

遮帕麻开口笑笑，
说出话来像蜜甜：
"从今以后交朋友，
不知你愿不愿？"

腊訇说话口水溅：
"要交朋友我为大，
天地归我管，
事事要听我的话。"

遮帕麻说：
"我们来比智斗法，
你要赢了就尊你为大，
我要胜了我就管天下。"

魔王没有话讲，
两个相邀到山前。
山坳里有棵花桃树，
枝繁叶茂花儿鲜。

When Zhepa Ma went to Lahong's home,
the demon rolled his eyes without speaking,
showing a ghostly look and full of anger,
neither invited him to sit nor service him tea.

Zhepa Ma smiled,
his words sweet as honey:
"How about becoming friends from now on,
would you like this idea?"

Lahong answered with saliva spattering:
"I must be in charge if we are friends.
I will be in charge of the sky and the earth
and everything else."

Zhepa Ma said:
"Let's have a competition of our mental powers,
and if you win, you will be in charge,
but if I win, I will govern the world."

The demon had nothing to say,
so they agreed to meet in front of a mountain.
where a peach tree was in a mountain col,
with luxuriant leaves and fresh flowers.

腊匐上前去，
念了一串咒语，
又掐动手指头，
桃枝顿时叶蔫花枯。

他张开血口哈哈大笑，
洋洋得意地自夸：
"生灵死活我掌握，
谁的神通还能比我大？"

遮帕麻说：
"腊匐且莫夸，
谁有真本领，
要让枯枝再发芽。"

腊匐连连摇头：
"枯枝怎能再发芽，
枯花怎能再开放！
起死回生我无法。"

遮帕麻念动咒语，
又端来一碗泉水，
含一口清水喷花桃，
一眨眼工夫雨霏霏。

Lahong walked up to the tree,

recited some spell,

also pinched his fingers,

and suddenly the branches withered, so did the leaves and

blossoms.

Bursting into laugher,

he boasted:

"I control life and death,

so whose power can be greater than mine?"

Zhepa Ma replied:

"Don't boast, Lahong,

because the real power

is in making the dead branches sprout again."

Lahong shook his head vigorously:

"Withered branches cannot sprout again

and withered flowers cannot blossom again!

I cannot bring the dead back to life."

Zhepa Ma recited some spell,

brought over a bowl of spring water,

and sprayed a mouthful of water onto the peach tree,

creating an instant gentle drizzle.

花桃重吐新芽，
枝头再开白花。
腊訇脸色像黄蜡，
目瞪口呆变成了哑巴。

The peach tree sprouted again

and white flowers bloomed at the end of the branches.

His face looking like yellow wax,

Lahong stood there dumbfounded.

第二折　斗梦

腊旬不服气，
又打鬼主意：
"今日斗法不算数，
明日斗梦比高低。

"做了好梦交好运，
做了噩梦不吉利。
谁该坐天下，
梦中看天意。"

遮帕麻上山顶，
腊旬下山箐：
各做各的梦，
约定明日到山腰谈梦境。

遮帕麻准时到山腰，
心里高兴脸带笑；
腊旬垂头丧气，
心中像火烧。

遮帕麻说：
"我梦见太阳红彤彤，
山中泉水照人影，
树叶树枝青葱葱。"

124

II. Competition of Dreams

Lahong was not convinced

and thought of another devilish idea:

"Today's competition does not count,

and let's see the result of the dream competition tomorrow.

"Good dreams mean good luck,

and nightmares mean bad luck.

Whoever rules the whole world

will be decided by the will of Heaven revealed in the

dream."

Zhepa Ma went up to the mountaintop,

while Lahong went down to the valley:

They each would dream their own dreams,

but agreed to talk about the dreams on the hillside the next

day.

Zhepa Ma arrived at the hillside on time,

happy in the heart and smiling on the face;

Lahong was distraught,

with the heart burning like fire.

Zhepa Ma said:

"I dreamed the sun that was red,

the spring water that was so clear that it reflected people,

and the leaves and branches that were green and lush."

腊訇有气无力地说：
"我梦见山顶黑乎乎，
箐沟流出黄泥水，
枯树枯枝光秃秃。"

遮帕麻做好梦，
腊訇做噩梦。
腊訇又输了，
遮帕麻又赢了。

腊訇耍赖说：
"昨天的梦不算数。
我上山顶你下箐，
再梦一回定输赢。"

遮帕麻点点头：
"再比一次也不怕。"
腊訇上了山顶，
遮帕麻来到山下。

第二天清早，
腊訇来找遮帕麻，
脸孔阴沉沉，
说话结结巴巴：

Lahong said feebly:

"I dreamed the mountaintop that was black,

the valley that had yellow mud water flowing,

and the tree that was bare with withered branches."

Zhepa Ma had a good dream,

while Lahong had a nightmare.

Lahong lost again,

and Zhepa Ma won again.

Lahong said shamelessly:

"Yesterday's dreams do not count.

I should go up to the mountaintop and you go down to the

valley

to dream again to decide who wins."

Zhepa Ma nodded:

"I am not afraid to compete again."

Lahong went up to the mountaintop,

while Zhepa Ma came to the foot of the mountain.

The next morning,

Lahong came to find Zhepa Ma,

his face gloomy,

his speech stuttering:

"我梦中不见太阳面，
只见山崩地倒塌，
满山枯藤挂老树，
浑水泥浆淌山洼。"

遮帕麻说：
"我梦见太阳亮堂堂，
绿树枝头喜鹊叫，
洼里泉水清汪汪。"

腊訇又输了，
脸色难看，像死了爹娘，
勉强答应交朋友，
再也不说要尊他为王。

"I did not see the sun in my dream,
but only the landslide and sinkholes,
with old trees and dead vines all over the mountains,
and mud flowing through all mountain valleys."

Zhepa Ma said:
"I dreamed of the bright sun,
magpies chirping on the green tree branches,
spring water in the valley limpid and clear."

Lahong lost again,
looking sad as if his parents died,
agreeing reluctantly to be friends,
and never want to be the king.

第三折　智伏腊匈

遮帕麻和腊匈交了朋友，
胸中有了战胜魔王的计谋。
回家提上赶山鞭，
高高兴兴往山上走。

白菌子红菌子撒入松林，
甜鸡枞香鸡枞撒在山头。
砍棵竹子抬回家，
编成竹筐和竹篓。

雷雨过后出鸡枞，
遮米麻拾回一满篓。
桑姑尼生火来烹煮，
加了盐，调了油。

送碗香喷喷的鸡枞给腊匈，
让他美味下米酒。
鸡枞香，米酒甜，
腊匈吃了直点头：

"美味鸡枞甜透心，
这样的好东西哪里有？
遮帕麻啊快快告诉我，
有福同享才算好朋友。"

Ⅲ. Taking Down Lahong by Strategy

Having made friends with Lahong,
Zhepa Ma made a plan to defeat the demon.
Picking up the mountain-driving whip,
he went home walking happily up to the mountain.

White and red mushroom seeds were sprinkled in the pine
forest,
as sweet and fragrant chanterelle seeds, on the mountaintop.
A bamboo pole was cut and carried home
for weaving a bamboo basket and a bamboo bucket.

After a thunderstorm, the chanterelle mushroom grew,
so Zhemi Ma went and picked a basketful.
Sangguni started the fire,
added the salt, and mixed the oil dressing.

A bowl of fried chanterelle mushroom was sent to Lahong
to be served with the rice wine.
Tasting the delicious chanterelle mushroom and sweet rice
wine,
Lahong kept nodding:

"This tasty chanterelle dish,
where can such a good thing be found?
Zhepa Ma, ah, tell me quickly,
since good friends share weal and woe."

131

遮帕麻真高兴，
凶恶的腊訇已上钩：
"爱吃只管上山采，
这种美味遍山有。"

遮帕麻提起赶山鞭，
拔脚就往山上走，
踏遍山头和山沟，
撒下毒菌鬼见愁①。

遮米麻左肩挎竹筐，
遮米麻右肩挎竹篓，
去约腊訇家的小妖精：
"想吃鸡枞跟我走。"

遮米麻拾到毒菌放进竹筐，
遮米麻拾到鸡枞放进竹篓。
竹筐眼大装不住，
漏了一地鬼见愁。

小妖精拾起毒菌说：
"你的筐子漏呀，老奶奶！"
遮米麻装作慷慨的样子：
"漏在地上的你只管顺手捡。

---

① 鬼见愁：一种名为无患子的有毒植物。

Zhepa Ma was very happy,

because the vicious Lahong had taken the bait:

"If you like chanterelle, just go up the mountain and pick

this delicacy that is all over the mountain."

Zhepa Ma then picked up the mountain-driving whip,

walked up the mountain right afterward,

and sprinkled on all mountaintops and valleys

poisonous mushroom soapberry①.

Carrying the bamboo basket on the left shoulder

and the bamboo bucket on the right one,

Zhemi Ma went to invite Lahong's little vixen:

"If you want to eat chanterelle mushroom, come with me."

Zhemi Ma put the picked poisonous mushrooms in the
basket

and the chanterelle mushroom in the bucket.

The bamboo basket had holes too big to hold the
mushroom,

so she dropped soapberries all over the place.

The little vixen picked up the poisonous mushrooms and said:

"Your basket is leaking, Granny!"

Pretending to be generous, Zhemi Ma replied:

"You can have what has been dropped on the ground."

---

① soapberry: it is a poisonous plant.

遮米麻拾了一背甜鸡枞，
小妖精捡了一背鬼见愁。
各自回到各的家，
腊訇见了口水直流。

等不得菌子煮熟，
腊訇就张开血盆大口，
一阵狼吞虎咽，
连淹带汤吃了个够。

腊訇吃了鬼见愁，
肚子疼得冷汗流，
倒在地上直打滚，
好像一万只老虎在吼。

腊訇家的妖精三天不出门，
腊訇家的房顶三天不冒烟，
不知腊訇死硬了没有？
遮帕麻派水牛去查看。

水牛刚出门，
天热淌大汗，
泡在水塘里，
忘了去察看。

Zhemi Ma picked up a bucket of sweet chanterelle mushroom,

whereas the little vixen picked up a pack of soapberries.

They each went home,

and Lahong, seeing the mushroom, had his mouth watering.

Before the mushroom was well cooked,

Lahong opened his bloody mouth,

wolfing down for quite some time

and having already had his fill of everything including the soup.

Having had soapberries,

Lahong had a stomachache so bad that he was wet with cold sweat,

fell to the ground, rolling around,

and roared like ten thousand tigers would.

For three days Lahong's little vixen did not leave the house,

and Lahong's chimney saw no smoke.

Was Lahong dead yet?

Zhepa Ma sent the buffalo to check it out.

As soon as the buffalo went out of the door,

it got hot and sweaty,

so it decided to soak in the pond,

and forgot to check on Lahong.

遮帕麻一气穿了牛鼻子,
牛脖子上把弯担架:
"活着去犁田,
死了剐干巴!"

又派黄牛去察看,
黄牛来到半路上,
看见一片甘庶林,
贪吃又把差事忘。

遮帕麻气坏了,
瞪着眼睛骂:
"瘦时挨鞭抽,
胖了用刀杀!"

又派马儿去察看,
马儿走进腊訇家,
看见一摊草,
只顾把滚打。

遮帕麻揪住马尾骂:
"让人骑着跑,
罚去驮东西,
鞍子背上架!"

招来两只小麻雀,
展翅飞到腊訇家。
看见魔王死硬了,
回来告诉遮帕麻。

Zhepa Ma angrily pierced the buffalo's nose
and placed the yoke around its neck:
"You plow the fields when you are alive
and be served as beef when you are dead!"

Then the cow was sent to check on Lahong,
But when halfway
the cow saw a field of sugarcane,
it indulged in it too much to remember the errand.

Zhepa Ma was so furious
that he cursed with bulging eyeballs:
"You will be whipped when you are thin,
and killed when you are fat!"

Then a horse was sent to check on Lahong,
but as soon as the horse walked into Lahong's yard
and saw the hay,
it cared only about rolling in the hay.

Zhepa Ma grabbed the horse's tail and scolded:
"You will have people ride on you
and carry things as your punishments,
with a saddle on your back!"

Then two little sparrows were called
to spread their wings and fly to Lahong's house.
Seeing the demon dead hard,
they came back and told Zhepa Ma.

喜讯乐坏遮帕麻，
高高兴兴对麻雀说道：
"饿了谷囤头上吃，
天黑就住屋檐下。"

又派两只小老鼠，
飞快跑到腊訇家。
老鼠闻见魔王尸臭了，
咬回两个手指甲。

消息喜坏遮帕麻，
高高兴兴对老鼠说道：
"谷囤米囤脚下吃，
墙脚打洞去安家。"

出来一只大苍蝇，
嗡嗡飞到腊訇家，
在魔王鼻孔耳孔里下卵，
在魔王眼珠上搓脚。

飞回告诉遮帕麻，
遮帕麻对苍蝇说道：
"甑子头上你去吃，
饭桌上面任你抓。"

腊訇的尸体臭气冲天，
狗去咬他的心，
猪去拱他的肝，
七零八散，碎成万段。

The good news made Zhepa Ma very happy,
so he said to the sparrow joyfully:
"Eat the grain in the barn when you are hungry
and live under the eaves of the roof when it is dark."

then two little mice were sent,
who ran at the flying speed to Lahong's house.
They smelled the rotten corpse of the demon,
bit off two fingernails, and carried them back.

The good news delighted Zhepa Ma very much,
so he spoke to the mice happily:
"Eat at the foot of where the grains are stored,
make holes at the foot of the wall as your home."

A big fly came,
buzzingly flew into Lahong's house,
laid eggs in the nostrils and ears of the demon,
and rubbed its feet on the demon's eye balls.

On its return, the fly told Zhepa Ma about all this,
and Zhepa Ma said to the fly:
"Eat on top of the steamer,
and grab any food you like on the dining table."

The overwhelming stench of Lahong's corpse
attracted dogs who bit his heart,
and pigs who snouted at his liver.
His parts scattered and his corpse broke into pieces.

第四折 重整天地

腊訇凶狂野心大，
天理不容，自取身亡。
可他射上去的假太阳，
还散发着毒光。

森林还在冒着烟，
竹子还在倒着长，
山上的动物还在水里挣扎，
水里的鱼虾还困在山上。

遮帕麻拉开黄栗硬弓，
搭上九拿长的弩箭，
一箭射下假太阳，
天空不再喷毒焰。

天上出现了遮帕麻造的太阳，
天上出现了遮帕麻造的月亮，
太阳会出也会落，
月亮会升也会降。

遮帕麻挥舞赶山鞭，
把倒插的树木扶正，
把倒流的河水理顺，
把颠倒了的世界重新整顿。

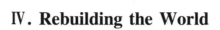

IV. Rebuilding the World

Lahong was viciously ambitious,

intolerable by the will of Heaven, deserving his death.

But the fake sun he shot up

still emitted toxic light.

The forest was still smoking;

the bamboo was still growing upside down;

the mountain animals were still struggling in the water;

the fish and shrimp in the water were still trapped on the

mountain.

Zhepa Ma drew a yellow chestnut wood bow,

and, with an arrow nine hands long,

shot down the fake sun,

and stopped the toxic flames from the sky.

The sky had the sun made by Zhepa Ma

and the moon made by Zhepa Ma,

the sun that could rise and set,

the moon that could rise and set.

Waving his mountain-driving whip,

Zhepa Ma righted the inverted trees,

reversed the backward flowing river,

and reset the upside down world.

水里的兽类放回山上，
山上的水族放回河里。
只有会打洞的穿山甲，
自愿留在山里。

遮帕麻甩动赶山鞭，
鞭树树成林，
鞭水水更清，
鱼儿回水鸟归林。

鱼儿回水得自由，
鸟儿归林传歌声。
英雄的遮帕麻啊，
理顺了阴阳挽救了生灵。

遮帕麻立下古老的规矩，
精心把世界管理。
百姓受苦他伤心，
百姓安宁他欢喜。

他派三十个神兵守山头，
临走时对他们讲：
"见毒蛇就要拔出长刀，
对鬼怪决不能手软。"

The beasts in the water returned to the mountains,

and the aquatic animals on the mountain were put back to
the river.

Only the hole-digging pangolin

volunteered to stay in the mountains.

Zhepa Ma wielded the mountain-driving whip,

whipping trees into forests,

whipping the water clearer,

whipping the fish back to the water and birds back to the
woods.

The fish were freed once returning to the river,

and the birds sang once returning to the woods.

Ah, hero Zhepa Ma

observed the Yin and Yang and saved the living beings.

Zhepa Ma set the ancient rules

for mindfully managing the world.

He was heartbroken when people suffered

and joyful when people lived peacefully.

He sent thirty heavenly soldiers to guard the mountaintops

and said to them before they left:

"Pull out your long sword when seeing the poisonous
viper,

and never be kind to monstrous ghosts."

他派三十员神将管村寨,
出发前一再对他们告诫:
"从今以后谁敢再作乱,
就跟腊訇同样下场!"

干涸了的池塘又流出清水,
逃出去的百姓又回到故乡。
烧光的草地又变绿,
枯死的鲜花又开放。

田里的谷子一年两次黄,
肥壮的牛羊满山冈。
大树高兴得招手,
河水高兴得歌唱。

最动听的调子是俄罗,
最美丽的花朵是攀枝花;
唱一支俄罗歌颂遮帕麻,
采一朵攀枝花献给遮米麻。

阿昌的子孙啊,
这就是遮帕麻和遮米麻的故事,
你们要牢牢记在心里,
世世代代传唱不歇。

He sent thirty heavenly generals to manage the villages
and repeatedly warned them before their departure:
"From now on, treat those who dare to cause trouble
the same as Lahong was treated!"

As the dried up ponds were refilled with clear water,
people who fled returned to their hometown.
The burnt grass turned green again,
and the dead flowers began to bloom again.

The millet in the field turned yellow twice a year,
and the fat cattle and sheep covered the mountain hills.
The big tree waved with joy,
and the river sang with delight.

The most melodious tune is Eluo,
and the most beautiful flower is the morning glory;
sing the Eluo in praise of Zhepa Ma,
and pick a morning glory for Zhemi Ma.

Ah, the offspring of Achang,
this is the story of Zhepa Ma and Zhemi Ma.
You should keep it firmly in mind,
and pass down the song from generation to generation.

遮帕麻和遮米麻的故事，
像天一样久长。
要知故事的来历，
请问月亮和太阳。

遮帕麻和遮米麻的故事，
像大地一样长存不衰。
要问故事出自哪里，
阿昌心底是它的故乡。

The story of Zhepa Ma and Zhemi Ma

is as long as the sky.

To learn about the origin of the story,

you can ask the moon and the sun.

The story of Zhepa Ma and Zhemi Ma

will last like the enduring earth.

If you want to know where the story comes from,

it is the hometown that is at the bottom of the hearts of all

Achang.

下篇：
达古达楞格莱标

Part 2:
Earliest Dagu and Daleng Legends

序　歌

乡亲们啊乡亲们，
我要把一支古歌来唱。
吃饭不要忘记种田的辛苦，
喝水不要忘记找水的艰难。
弹口弦不要忘记栽金竹的先辈，
吹芦笙不要忘记种葫芦的爹娘。
德昂人的古歌与大山一起诞生，
德昂人的历史像江河一样久长。
要细细地听啊，乡亲！
要牢牢地记啊，朋友！
莫要漏掉一句动听的话，
让古歌永远在心中珍藏。

Prelude

My fellow villagers, ah, my fellow villagers,

I'm going to sing an ancient song.

Eating, one should remember the hard work of the farming,

and drinking, one should remember the hard work to find the water.

Playing the harmonica, one should remember the grandparents who planted the golden bamboo,

and blowing the reed pipe, one should remember the parents who grew the gourds.

The ancient song of De'ang was born with the huge mountains,

and the history of the De'ang people is as long as the rivers.

Listen carefully, my fellow villagers!

Never forget, my friends!

Do not miss an important word,

and always treasure this ancient song with your heart.

第一部分　茶神下凡诞生人类

很古很古的时候，
大地一片浑浊。
水和泥巴搅在一起，
土和石头分不清楚。
没有鱼虫虾蟹，
没有麂子马鹿，
没有红花黄果，
没有绿草青树，
没有人的影子，
只有雷吼风呼……

天上美丽无比，
到处是茂盛的茶树，
翡翠一样的茶叶，
成双成对把枝干抱住。
茶叶是茶树的生命，
茶叶是万物的阿祖。
天上的日月星辰，
都是茶叶的精灵化出。

Chapter One   The God of Tea Determined to Descend

A long, long time ago,

the earth was a murky patch.

Water and mud were mixed together,

while dirt and stone were indistinguishable.

There were no fish, worms, shrimps or crabs,

no muntjacs, horses or deers,

no red flowers or yellow fruits,

no fresh grass and green trees,

not a shadow of the human being,

but only the roaring thunder and howling wind...

However, the sky was beautiful,

with lush tea bushes everywhere,

and emerald-like tea leaves in pairs

embracing the branches.

Tea leaves were the life of the tea bushes

and the ancestors of all things.

The sun, the moon and the stars in the sky

were all evolved from the spirit of the tea leaves.

金闪闪的太阳，
是茶果的光芒；
银灿灿的月亮，
是茶花在开放；
数不清的满天星星，
是茶叶眨眼闪光；
洁白的云彩，
是茶树的披纱飘散；
璀璨的晚霞，
是茶树的华丽衣裳……

天空五彩斑斓，
大地一片荒凉，
时时相望的天地啊，
为什么如此大不一样？
茶树在叹息，
茶树在冥想。
有一株茶树想得入迷，
忘记了饮食，
忘记了睡觉，
身体消瘦脸色发黄。

想呀想呀想呀想，
想了三百六十五天，
想了三百六十五年，
还是找不到答案。

The golden sun

was the light of the tea fruit;

the silvery moon

was the camellia in blossom;

the countless stars in the sky

were the bright blinking eyes of the tea leaves;

the spotless clouds

were the floating veil of the tea bushes;

the resplendent glow of the sunset

was the fancy dress of the tea bushes...

The splendent Heaven

and the desolate earth

always looked at each other,

but why were they so different?

The tea bushes were sighing

and pondering.

There was one tea bush so obsessed with the question

that it forgot to eat

or sleep

and became emaciated and sallow.

It thought over and over

for three hundred and sixty-five days,

and then for three hundred and sixty-five years,

but it could not find an answer.

茶树的怨气惊动了帕达然，
帕达然把茶树细盘：
"有什么疑问就对我讲，
千万不要胡思乱想，
一丝一毫的邪念，
也会带来万世难解的灾难。"

九百九十九棵茶树低下头，
九百九十九棵茶树愁眉展，
九百九十九棵茶树脸色发白，
九百九十九棵茶树发抖打战，
九百九十九棵茶树下跪磕头，
九百九十九棵茶树冷汗直淌。
只有一株焦黄的小茶树，
纹丝不动挺着腰杆，
抬头望着帕达然，
双眼凝视苦思想。

"尊敬的帕达然啊，
天上为什么繁华？
地下为什么凄凉？
我们为什么不能到地下生长？"
帕达然双掌合拢，
声音像洪钟一样：
"天下一片黑暗，
到处都是灾难，
下凡要受尽苦楚，
永远不能再回到天上。"

The resentment of the tea bush disturbed Padaran,

who asked the tea bush:

"Speak to me if you have any question,

but don't have a bee in your bonnet,

because the tiniest bit of evil thought

will bring an eternal calamity."

Nine hundred and ninety-nine tea bushes lowered their heads,

frowned,

turned pale,

trembled,

kneeled to kowtow,

and broke into a cold sweat,

but the one small tea bush, shriveled and sallow,

stood still with its back straight,

looking up at Padaran

and gazing in deep thought.

"Ah, respectable Padaran,

why is Heaven bustling with life?

Why is earth so bleak?

Why can't we grow on the earth?"

Padaran, putting his palms together,

sounded like a large bell:

"All under Heaven is darkness

and suffering,

so if you go down there, you will suffer all kinds of hardship

and can never return to Heaven."

帕达然的话像寒冷的冰霜，
打在每株茶树的身上。
帕达然的话像锋利的尖刀，
戳在每株茶树的心上。
帕达然的话像千斤铁棒，
砸在每株茶树的头上。
只有那株焦黄的茶树把话讲：
"尊敬的帕达然啊，
只要大地永远长青，
我愿意去把苦水尝。"

帕达然暗暗称赞，
为了开出繁华的世界，
再把小茶树来试探：
"小茶树啊要仔细想想，
地下有一万零一条冰河，
一万零一座火山，
一万零一种妖怪，
下去要遭一万零一次磨难。
不像天上清平吉乐，
不像天上舒适安康。"

Padaran's words were like the biting frost,

hitting on each tea bush.

Padaran's words were like sharp knives,

poking at the heart of every tea bush.

Padaran's words were like one thousand *jin* of iron,

striking on the head of every tea bush.

Only the shriveled and sallow tea bush said:

"Respectable Padaran,

as long as the earth flourishes for ever,

I am willing to taste all bitterness."

Padaran was impressed

but, for the development of a prosperous world,

decided to put the small tea bush to test:

"Think carefully, little tea bush,

about the ten thousand and one glaciers on the earth,

ten thousand and one volcanoes,

ten thousand and one kinds of monsters,

and ten thousand and one sufferings you will endure.

It is not as peaceful as in Heaven

or as comfortable."

小茶树眨了九十九次眼睛，
扳了九十九次指头，
想了又想把主意打定：
"尊敬的帕达然啊，
请你开恩，请你帮忙，
让我到天下去把路闯……"
小茶树的话还没有说完，
一阵狂风吹得天昏地暗。
狂风撕碎了小茶树的身子，
一百零二片叶子飘飘下凡。

天空雷电轰鸣，
大地沙飞石走，
天门像一个葫芦打开，
一百零二片茶叶在狂风中变化，
单数叶变成五十一个精悍伙子，
双数叶化为二十五对半美丽姑娘。
茶叶是德昂命脉，
有德昂的地方就有茶山。
神奇的传说流传到现在，
德昂人的身上还飘着茶叶的芳香。

The little tea bush blinked its eyes ninety-nine times,

counted with its fingers ninety-nine times,

thought it over and made up its mind:

"Respectable Padaran,

please allow me and help me

go to the earth and find my way..."

Before the little tea bush finished speaking,

a gust of violent wind blew the sky into darkness.

The violent wind tore up the body of the little tea bush

into one hundred and two leaves descending to the earth.

The sky roared with thunder and lightning,

and the earth had sands and stones flying,

the Gate of Heaven opening like a gourd split in half,

with one hundred and two tea leaves transforming in the wind,

odd numbered leaves turning into fifty-one vigorous young men,

even numbered leaves, twenty-five and a half pairs of pretty young women.

Tea is the lifeblood of the De'ang people,

who are wherever the tea mountains are.

The incredible legend has been passed on till now,

and the scent of the De'ang people is still the aroma of tea.

第二部分　光明与黑暗的斗争

一百零二个男女，
随着风沙在天空悠荡。
睁着眼睛看不见，
在黑暗中互相碰撞。
兄弟姐妹的哭声传到九天，
天上的亲友都来帮忙。
太阳搬出金钵，
月亮端出银盘，
星星射出光芒，
大地一片明亮。

一百零二个兄弟姐妹，
都朝金晃晃的地方俯瞰，
看到了无边无际的大地，
他们喜欢得互相拥抱，
他们喜欢得跳舞歌唱。
他们喜欢得眼泪洒到地上，
一滴眼泪划出一条小溪，
一串眼泪聚成小河流淌，
眼泪越聚越多，

Chapter Two　The War Between Light and Dark

A hundred and two brothers and sisters

were floating in the sky with the wind and sand.

They could see nothing though their eyes were open,

so bumped into each other in the dark.

When the cries of the brothers and sisters reached the Ninth

Heaven,

their friends and relatives in Heaven all came to help.

With the sun taking out its golden bowl,

the moon carrying out the silver plate,

and the stars giving out the light,

the earth were now shrouded in brightness.

When the one hundred and two brothers and sisters

looked down at the glittering golden place,

when they saw the boundless earth,

They became so joyful that they hugged each other,

danced and sang songs.

Their joyful tears spilled onto the earth,

each drop becoming a stream,

each string of tears gathering into a river,

and more and more tears

汇成大海汪洋。

到处是白浪滚滚，
到处是金涛闪闪，
兄弟姐妹随着风走，
哪里都没有落脚的地方。
飘到东边，波涛张开吃人的大嘴，
飘到西边，波涛举起杀人的利剑，
飘到南边，波涛挥舞打人的拳头，
飘到北边，波涛拍着饥饿的肚皮。
兄弟姐妹飘了一天又一天。
几万年还在空中飘荡。
几万年时间不算短暂，
天空渐渐暗淡：
太阳疲劳得打起瞌睡，
月亮疲劳得鼾声如雷，
星星疲劳得闭上眼睛。
一百零二个兄弟姐妹啊，
眼看着要跌下海洋，
到处是求救的嘶喊：
"天上的亲人啊再来帮忙，
我们又遇到了灾难。"

forming seas and oceans.

With white waves rolling everywhere,

gold waves shining everywhere,

the brothers and sisters drifted with the wind

and had no place to stay.

They met with the waves' human-eating mouth in the east,

the waves' human-killing swords in the west,

the waves' human-hitting fists in the south,

the waves' belly-slapping rage in the north.

The brothers and sisters drifted day after day.

For several tens of thousands of years, they drifted.

Tens of thousands of years were not a short time,

and the sky gradually began to dim:

with the sun dozing off with fatigue,

the moon snoring away like thunder,

and stars closing their eyes exhaustedly.

The one hundred and two brothers and sisters

were about to fall into the sea,

and their cry for help was heard everywhere:

"Our heavenly family, please help once more,

because we are in trouble once again."

呼声震动了天庭，
星星吓得直眨眼，
月亮吓得直打转，
太阳吓得忽明忽暗。
为了帮助下凡的兄弟姐妹，
日月星辰苦思冥想，
想了九千九百九十年，
还是赶不走凡间的黑暗。
想了九万九千九百九十年，
才有了一条妙计良方。

大家出来轮换照明，
团结齐心战胜黑暗。
太阳妹妹胆子小，
只好把白天承担。
月亮哥哥胆大身体壮，
带着小星弟弟守着晚上。
从此黑夜与白天分开，
从此大地才有了光明和温暖。

The cries shook Heaven so much

that the stars began to blink their eyes with fear,

the moon started spinning in terror,

and the sun flickered with fright.

To help their brothers and sisters,

the sun, the moon, and the stars thought hard,

yet for nine thousand nine hundred and ninety years,

they could not drive away the darkness from the earth,

But after ninety-nine thousand, nine hundred and ninety

years,

they finally came up with an excellent plan.

They took turn to light the world,

unified to overcome the darkness.

Since the younger sister, the sun, was timid,

she took the day shift.

As the older brother, the moon, was brave and strong,

he, together with the little brothers, the stars, took the

night shift.

From then on, the night and the day separated,

and the earth had light and warmth.

第三部分　战胜洪水和恶势力

黑暗刚刚消失，
洪水又泛滥，
五十一对兄妹呼声连天，
惊醒了智慧的帕达然。
他伸个懒腰把地震裂，
让水往地下流淌；
他打个哈欠唤来风，
让茶叶姐妹去施展力量。

堆得九万九千九百拿高的茶叶，
哗啦啦冲开天门两扇，
驾着清风驱洪水。
茶叶到处洪水退让，
洪水退处大地出现，
德昂山的泥土肥沃喷香，
因为它是祖先的身躯铺成。
每座山林都有吃的，
阿公阿祖留下了金仓。

茶叶把洪水越撵越远，

Chapter Three　Defeating the Flood and the Evil Forces

Just when the darkness was gone,

the flood happened,

and the cry of the fifty-one pairs of siblings

awakened the wise Padaran.

By stretching his back, he cracked the earth

to let the water flow under the ground;

by yawning, he called out the wind

to let the tea sisters exert their power.

Tea leaves piled ninety-nine thousand, nine hundred *fen* high,

and with the heavenly double-door bursting open,

they rode the breeze and drove off the flood.

Wherever the tea leaves arrived, floods receded,

and wherever the flood receded, the earth appeared,

the rich and fragrant earth, the soil of the De'ang mountains,

made by the bodies of the ancestors.

There was food in every mountain and forest,

the golden barns passed down from the great grandparents.

The tea leaves drove the flood water farther and farther away,

土地伸展得又宽又长。
兄弟姐妹正喜气洋洋,
帕达然出现在云天上:
"天要分南北西东,
才有方位四向;
地要有河谷山川,
才有寒热暖凉;
帕达然也有闷热的时候,
要留个洗澡的地方。"

茶叶停住脚步,
折头返回天上。
他们精疲力竭,
步子越来越慢,
有力气的慢慢赶路,
没力气的躺在路上。
茶叶越撒越多,
大地越积越厚,
回到西天脚下,
天门已经关上。

从此,大地留下九湖十八海,
那是帕达然洗澡的地方。
从此,大地留下千河万江,
那是茶叶姐妹的泪水在淌。
从此,挨近海的土地平展展,
离海远的地方突起座座高山。
离海最远的西天下,
是世界上最高的地方。

and the land stretched out wider and longer.

Just when the brothers and sisters were in high spirits,

Padaran appeared in the sky:

"The sky must have north, south, west and east,

so that there are the four directions;

the earth must have valleys and mountains,

so that there are coldness, hotness, warmth and coolness;

Padaran also feel sultry sometimes,

so there should be a place for bathing."

The tea leaves stopped going forward

and began to head back to Heaven.

Exhausted,

they walked more and more slowly,

with some still strong enough to move slowly,

while others too weak to walk lying by the roads.

More and more the tea leaves were scattered around,

and the earth became thicker and thicker with tea leaves,

so by the time they reached the foot of the western Heaven,

the Heavenly Gate had already been closed.

Since then, the earth has had nine lakes and eighteen seas,

where Padaran bathes himself.

Since then, the earth has had thousands of rivers,

the running tears of the tea-leave sisters.

Since then, the land near the sea was open and flat,

while the land far from the sea stood mountains rising high.

And the Western Heaven, the farthest away from the sea,

is the highest place in the world.

地下洪水退尽，
天空一片瓦蓝，
兄弟姐妹高兴地向下张望，
新生的大地奇形怪状：
到处是恶魔发狂，
四种魔鬼一个模样，
三个头六只手，
眼睛四只脚八双。
刚刚生出的大地，
在妖魔的脚下遭殃。

为了大地清平安康，
兄弟姐妹与妖魔恶战。
红魔吐出烈火熊熊，
白魔喷出浓雾蒙蒙，
黑魔布下瘟疫阵阵，
黄魔撒出乌毒茫茫。
烈火烧身雾迷眼，
瘟疫笼罩毒穿心，
前面的弟兄倒在地下，
后面的姐妹逃回天上。

As floods subsided on the earth,

and the sky turned blue like a glazed tile,

the brothers and sisters looked down happily

only to find the strange state of the new earth:

Monsters were going mad everywhere,

and all the four kinds of them were in one form,

each with three heads and six hands,

four eyes and eight pairs of feet.

The newly born earth

was suffering from the reign of the monsters.

For the peace and well-being of the earth,

brothers and sisters began to fight the monsters.

The red monster spat fire roaring,

the white one exhaled fog thickening,

the black one started plagues repeatedly,

and the yellow one cast poison expansively.

With the fire burning the bodies, the fog blinding the eyes,

the plague inflicted upon them, and the poison piercing

their hearts,

the young men in front fell to the ground,

and the sisters in the back fled back to Heaven.

姐妹为弟兄着急，
咬破了指头，
咬碎了牙齿，
眼睛里血泪汪汪。
要亲骨肉脱灾消难，
先扫除凶恶的魔王。
请新月化作银弓，
求太阳赐给金箭，
从天门搬来清风，
与星星借得刺芒。

彩霞托着姐妹，
日月星辰助战。
金箭把烈火射灭，
清风把浓雾驱散，
刺芒把乌毒溶化，
瘟疫在闪电中消亡。
四个妖魔被打败，
身子分成十六半。
大地像水洗过一样清净，
天空像玛瑙般明亮。

The sisters were so worried for their brothers,

that they bit their fingers bleeding

and their teeth broken,

and their eyes were brimming with bloody tears.

To free their own brothers from suffering,

they must first wipe out the fierce monsters.

They asked that the new moon transform into a silver bow,

requested the sun to grant them a golden arrow,

invited the breeze from the Heavenly Gate,

and borrowed prickly thorns from the stars.

The sisters were carried by the rosy clouds

and fought side by side with the sun, the moon and the

stars.

The golden arrow put out the fire,

the breeze dispelled the thick fog,

the prickly thorns rendered the poison useless,

and lightning eradicated the plague.

The four monsters were defeated,

their bodies divided into sixteen parts.

The earth became as clean as water,

and the sky was as bright as agate.

姐妹把弟兄呼唤，
声音像山泉一样动听。
姐妹把弟兄抚摸，
感情像烈火一样滚烫。
弟兄们有了热气，
弟兄们睁开了眼，
弟兄们伸开了手，
弟兄们直起了腰。
弟兄们活起来了，
姐妹们喜气洋洋。

姐妹们跳起庆贺的舞蹈，
弟兄们把再生的歌欢唱。
唱歌跳舞的人啊，
忘记了四个魔王。
地下的魔尸又作恶，
飞起来搅得天昏地暗。
弟兄姐妹又被包围，
他们赤手空拳勇敢迎战。
对失败的魔鬼决不要饶恕，
苦难换来的教训永不能忘。

When the sisters called for the brothers,

their voices were as pleasant as that of the mountain spring.

When the sisters touched the brothers,

their hearts felt like the burning fire.

The brothers were revived by the heat,

opened their eyes,

stretched out their hands,

and straightened their backs.

The brothers came back to life,

which delighted the sisters.

The sisters began to dance the celebratory dance,

while the brothers started to sing the rebirth song.

People who were singing and dancing

forgot about the four monsters.

The four monsters on the earth did evil again,

flying up in the air and blackening the sky and the earth.

The brothers and sisters were surrounded again,

but they fought bravely with their bare hands.

Showing no mercy to the defeated monsters,

they must not forget the lessons learned by suffering hardships.

弟兄在地下还击，
姐妹飞在空中助战。
打了三万年，
魔尸打碎了一个；
打了六万年，
魔尸打碎了一双；
打了九万年，
魔尸才统统死亡。
清平的大地不能再动乱，
欢乐的时光不能再暗淡。
弟兄在地下挖坑，
姐妹把魔尸埋葬。
黑白红黄的大地，
就是魔尸浸染。

The brothers fought on the ground,

and the sisters helped with the fight in the air.

After fighting for thirty thousand years,

one monster was smashed to pieces;

after fighting for sixty thousand years,

a couple more monsters were smashed to pieces;

after fighting for ninty thousand years,

all the monsters were dead.

The peaceful earth should not be disturbed again,

and the happy times should not be darkened again.

The brothers dug the graves on the ground,

where the sisters buried the monsters' corpses.

The black, white, red and yellow colors of the earth

were soaked with and dyed by the monsters' corpses.

第四部分　百花百果的由来与腰箍的来历

云彩在空中自由地飘，
姐妹们踩着云彩遨游。
高兴时唱歌跳舞，
累了就在云彩上躺。
弟兄们踏着的大地十分可怜，
裸露着身子光着臂膀。
天空的云变幻七彩，
土地怎么能没有衣裳！
兄弟姐妹都很苦恼，
只好再回到天上求援。
智慧的帕达然教给一句话，
舍掉身子大地就有衣裳。

兄弟姐妹顿时醒悟，
告别了帕达然又下凡。
割下身上的皮肉，
搓碎了撒到地上。
活蹦乱跳的皮肉，
把千山万水铺绿。
大的变树，小的成草，

Chapter Four　The Origin of Flowers and Fruits and the Waist Band

The clouds floating freely in the air,

carrying the sisters to roam around.

They sang and danced when happy

and lay down on the clouds when tired.

The earth the brothers standing on was pitiful,

naked with bare limbs.

The clouds in the sky changed colors,

but the earth had no clothes to wear!

The brothers and sisters were all troubled by this

and had to turn to Heaven again for help.

The wise Padaran gave them a tip,

sacrifice your bodies and the earth would have clothes.

The brothers and sisters understood instantly,

so they said goodbye to Padaran and return to the earth again.

They cut off the flesh of their bodies,

crumbled the pieces and sprinkled them on the ground.

The live and kicking flesh

carpeted all the mountains and rivers green.

Larger pieces became big trees while smaller ones, grass,

细细的肉筋变成青藤爬上树。
从此大地一派生机,
到处郁郁葱葱。

一丈高的弟兄缩成五尺半的郎儿,
胖墩墩的姐妹变成瘦削的姑娘。
弟兄们走遍东南西北,
姐妹们飞遍平坝高山,
树木草藤低头迎接,
把茶叶兄妹叫作生身爹娘。

弟兄们走啊走,
走过的路只有土地说得清。
姐妹们飞啊飞,
飞过的地方只有蓝天讲得明。
弟兄们顾不得汗水如雨下,
姐妹们忘记了鲜血似水淌。
汗水和鲜血滴过的草木上,
一朵朵鲜花迎风开放。
大地从此有了笑脸,
一年四季都有绿叶红花装扮。

兄弟姐妹把鲜美的颜色撒给百花,
百花盛开争艳斗芳,
有红有白有紫有黄,

with thin tendons turning into green vines climbing the
trees.

From then on, the earth was full of life
and was verdant everywhere.

The ten-foot brothers shrank into five and a half *chi* young
men,

and the plump sisters slimmed down.

The brothers traveled in all directions,

and the sisters flew over the flatlands and high mountains,

The trees and vines bowed their heads to greet them

and called tea brothers and sisters their parents.

The brothers walked so much

that only the land could tell how far they had walked.

The sisters flew so much

that only the blue sky could tell how far they had flown.

The brothers could not care about the rain-like sweat,

and the sisters, the blood like running-water.

The grass and trees, dripped with sweat and blood,

yielded flowers blooming in the wind.

Since then the earth has had smiling faces

with green leaves and red flowers all year around.

When the brothers and sisters sprinkled bright colors on the
flowers,

all flowers fully blossomed, rivaling in beauty and fragrance,

red, white, purple and yellow,

有大有小有浓有淡。
留给茶花的颜色普通平常，
碧绿的花托，
嫩黄的花蕊，
洁白的花瓣。
牺牲自己成全大家的美德，
永远受到世人的称赞。
鲜艳的百花开了又谢，
一年一度不久长。
素白的茶花结茶果，
茶果落地传子孙。
兄弟请来喜雨和甘露，
姐妹请来太阳和月亮，
茶果把身子碾成粉末，
乘着和风撒到百花上。

茶粉到处花结果，
百种果子不一般。
有大有小有扁有长，
有甜有酸有肉有浆。
美丽的样子给百果，
鲜艳的颜色给百果，
可口的味道给百果，
茶果只留下苦涩的味道和本样。
吃着香甜的桃李菠萝，
莫把结籽的茶果遗忘。

big, small, rich and light.

The colors left for the camellia were ordinary,

with the dark green receptacle,

the bright yellow stamens,

and the pure white flowers.

The virtue of sacrificing themselves for the good of all

is praised by the world forever.

The bright flowers bloomed and faded,

not lasting long each year.

The plain white camellia could bear fruits,

which passed on to the posterity once falling to the ground.

The brothers invited the rain and the dew,

and sisters invited the sun and the moon,

as the fruits of the tea ground themselves into pollen

to spread onto the flowers by the gentle wind.

The tea pollen produced flowers and fruits everywhere,

the fruits that were varied and quite different.

They were big or small, flat or long,

sweet or sour, meaty or pulpy.

Having given the attractive appearances to other fruits,

bright colors to other fruits,

delicious taste to other fruits,

the tea leaves were left with the bitter taste and the rustic
looks.

When eating sweet peaches, plums and pineapples,

do not forget the tea fruit that produced the seeds for all.

茶叶的儿孙世代延续，
绿草盖着平坝的胸膛，
大树保护山冈的脊梁，
高高的龙竹把山谷陪伴。
茶叶兄妹过着快乐的日子，
累了在白云上歇脚，
热了在青树下乘凉，
饿了把甜美的果子品尝。

好心的人自古就多磨难，
幸福日子过了九万年。
一阵黑风横扫大地，
把相亲相爱的兄妹吹散。
姐妹被送上高空，
弟兄被打在地下，
姐妹弯酸了腰下不了地，
弟兄跳疼了脚上不了天。
黑风狞笑着走了，
云天隔断的兄妹只能远远相望。

The posterity of the tea leaves survived for generations,

on earth where green grass covered the chest of the flatland,

the big trees protected the vertebral columns of the mountain hills,

and the tall dragon bamboos accompanied the valleys.

The tea-leaf brothers and sisters lived happily,

taking breaks, when tired, on the white clouds,

cooling off, when hot, under the green trees,

and tasting, when hungry, the sweet fruits.

Since ancient times, the good-hearted had suffered more,

so their happy days lasted for only ninety thousand years.

Then a burst of black wind swept across the earth,

which blew away brothers and sisters who loved each other.

With the sisters having been sent high into the sky

and the brothers, thrown to the ground,

the sisters bent over hard but could not reach the ground,

and the brothers jumped up hard but could not reach the sky.

The sinister wind left with a grim sneer,

leaving the brothers and sisters looking at each other from afar.

云中的姐妹望地下，
深情的眼睛泪汪汪：
难分难舍的哥哥哟，
江河里流着共同的泪水，
草木上附着共同的皮肉，
百花里洒着共同的血汗，
青石上留着共同的誓言，
竹蓬下埋着共同的理想。
再死再生九万次，
也要紧紧贴在你身上。

地下的弟兄望天上，
忽首不动情意长：
骨肉相连的姐妹哟，
早上望你望得眼睛花，
白天望你望得碎断肠，
黄昏望你望得面憔悴，
晚上望你望得心发慌，
三更望你望得脖子僵。
再生再死九万次，
也要像茶花茶果命相连。

兄弟姐妹两分离，
惊动帕达然走出天门：
"天地相通九十九条路，
懒惰的人望空叹。"

The sisters in the clouds looked down at the earth,

their tears welling up in their affectionate eyes:

We and our dear brothers

have shed tears that flow in the same river,

have had flesh that came from the same bushes,

have poured our sweat onto the same flowers,

have carved our vow on the same rock,

have buried our ideal under the same bamboo canopy.

Even if we will die and relive ninty thousand times,

we must stick together.

When the brothers on the earth looked up to the sky,

they stood still with deepest affections:

Our sisters by the same ancestry,

we look for you in the morning till our vision is blurry,

look for you during the day till we are heart-broken,

look for you at dusk till we look sick,

look for you in the evening till our hearts are flustering,

look for you at midnight till our necks are stiff.

Even if we will die and relive thity thousand times,

we must be together as are the tea flowers and tea fruits.

The separation of the brothers and the sisters

again had to trouble Padaran to walk out of the Heavenly

Gate:

"With ninety-nine roads between Heaven and the earth,

only the lazy do nothing but sigh and stare at the sky."

189

帕达然点出一句话，
打开兄妹心里四面窗。
弟兄往上纵跳抓亲人，
姐妹朝下把云彩按。
不知过了多少年，
兄妹还是隔云望。

姐妹把彩云搓成线，
要拉弟兄上云端。
弟兄搬土堆高台，
要接姐妹下凡尘。
云绳搓得九百丈，
风吹线断心血飘。
台子堆得九百丈，
雨打泥散白枉然。
堆台搓绳一万年，
还是姐妹叫来弟兄喊。
弟兄走到山尖，
爬到高高的大树上，
朝天伸出龙竹，
兄妹的手还是隔着八百丈。
再搬来十八凹的青石砌脚台，
还是挨不着心爱的姑娘。
想到的办法都用尽，
九十九条路不知在何方？

One hint from Padaran

opened the windows of the siblings' hearts.

The brothers jumped up high to catch the sisters,

who tried hard to press the clouds down.

But many years had passed,

the brothers and sisters were still separated by the clouds.

The sisters then twisted the clouds into a rope,

hoping to pull their brothers up the clouds.

The brothers built a high platform with dirt,

hoping to help their sisters come down to the earth.

When the cloud rope was made to nine-hundred *zhang* long,

a gale of wind blew the rope broken and together with all

effort.

When the platform was built to nine-hundred *zhang* high,

a pouring rain collapsed the platform together with all the

work.

It had been ten-thousand years of platform- and rope-

making,

but the sisters and brothers were still calling for each other.

The brothers walked up to the mountaintop,

where they climbed up tall trees

and stretched out the dragon bamboo poles towards the sky,

but their hands were still eight hundred *zhang* apart.

They then carried over the *shibaao* rock footrest,

but the brothers still could not reach the beloved sisters.

They have tried every way they could think of,

but where were the ninety-nine roads?

191

弟兄们耗尽力气，
在森林中静静歇息。
最小的兄弟最贪玩，
扯一根青藤绕成圈。
放在地下套着小草，
左右丢去套着树枝。
向上抛去套得着低低的白云，
藤圈撬开了小弟达楞的心窗，
他用尽全力往天上丢，
藤圈套着小妹亚楞落地上。

达楞套下亚楞的奇迹，
提醒了躺着的弟兄。
劈开荆棘扯青藤，
编成结实的藤圈。
五十个藤圈抛上天，
套下二十五对姑娘。
神奇的藤圈搭起通天路，
拆散的骨肉又团圆。
开天辟地第一回，
五十一对男女结成双。

The brothers were exhausted

and took a quiet break in the woods.

The youngest brother who was the most carefree

picked the green vines and made them into a wreath.

He threw it around the top of some grass

and tossed it left and right around the tree branches.

Thrown up, the vine wreath could catch the low white
clouds

and gave little brother Daleng an idea,

so, with all his strength, he threw the vine wreath into the
sky

and caught and brought down little sister Yaleng to the
ground.

The miracle of Daleng catching Yaleng by the vine wreath

gave the other brothers lying on the ground the idea.

Cutting the thorny bushes to collect the green vines,

they wove the sturdy vine rings.

When fifty vine rings were thrown into the sky,

the twenty-five pairs of sisters were caught and brought
down.

The miraculous vine rings formed a path to the sky

and reunited the separated siblings.

For the first time in history,

fifty one pairs of brothers and sisters matched as fifty one
couples.

第五部分 先祖的诞生和
各民族的繁衍

兄妹成双成对,
大地增光生辉。
兄妹到处游玩,
走遍四面八方。
兄妹到江河里嬉戏,
静静的河水过于孤单,
把泥巴撒进水里,
变成鱼虾蟹蚌……
流水有了伙伴,
日夜奔腾欢畅。

兄妹来到山林,
草木诉说白天的冷清,
岩石讲述夜晚的凄凉,
乞求兄妹开恩,
让大家都有伙伴。
兄妹把泥巴撒进山洞,

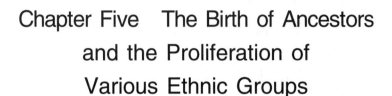

Chapter Five　The Birth of Ancestors and the Proliferation of Various Ethnic Groups

With brothers and sisters matched as couples,

the earth began to shine with radiance.

The brothers and sisters traveled around,

in all directions.

When they played in the river,

they found the quiet river too lonely,

so they sprinkled mud into the water,

the mud that transformed into fish, shrimp, crab, and

clam...

After the running river had partners,

the river began to run day and night with delight.

When they went to the mountains,

the grass and trees told them about their lonely day,

and the rocks told them about their desolate night,

begging for help from the siblings

to find them partners.

The brothers and sisters scattered mud in the mountain

caves,

满山坡众兽欢跳。
兄妹把泥巴撒遍山林，
草木中群鸟飞翔。
百兽围着兄妹起舞，
百鸟绕着兄妹歌唱。
歌声拨动兄妹的心弦，
舞步推着兄妹的脚板。
姐妹唱得喘不过气，
兄弟跳得满头大汗。
为了玩得更加舒畅，
五十个弟兄解下姐妹的藤圈。
只有最小的妹妹亚楞，
忙着倾诉爱情把藤圈遗忘。

兄妹越唱越跳越喜欢，
歌舞中出现了奇怪的景象。
五十个姐妹身变轻，
随着清风上天庭。
亚楞腰上箍藤圈，
拉着达楞两相亲。
腰上箍着藤圈的姑娘靠得住，
至今还流传在德昂山。

and various beasts appeared on the slope jumping with joy.

The brothers and sisters scattered mud all over the mountain

forests,

and birds emerged flying among the grass and trees.

The siblings were surrounded by dancing beasts

and singing birds.

Their heartstrings were struck by the songs,

and their feet were moved by the dancing steps.

The sisters sang till they were breathless,

and the brothers danced till their sweat pouring.

To have an even more enjoyable time,

fifty brothers untied their sister's vine ring.

Only the youngest sister, Yaleng,

was busy talking with Daleng and forgot about the vine

ring.

The more siblings sang and danced, the happier they

became,

but a strange scene appeared as they sang and danced.

The fifty sisters became lighter

and returned to Heaven with the breeze.

Yaleng with the vine ring on her waist

and Daleng, holding hands, got married.

The young woman with the vine ring around the waist is

reliable,

a saying that is still heard today around Mount De'ang.

五十个姐姐上了天，
五十个哥哥哭断肠，
只剩达楞和亚楞，
岩洞深处度时光。
太阳出了又落，
月亮缺了又圆，
达楞和亚楞有了儿子和姑娘，
世代繁衍人口兴旺。
小岩洞挤不下住进大岩房，
普天下的岩洞都被人挤满。
要叫子孙生存，
亚楞和达楞仔细商量。
砍来竹木搭屋架，
割来茅草盖起房。
水里引来鸡鹅鸭，
山中牵回猪牛羊，
百草结籽来报恩，
人类从此有食粮。
过着欢乐的日子，
切莫忘记祖先创业的艰难。

达楞和亚楞的子孙，
住满了平坝和高山，
歌颂祖宗的恩情，

The fifty sisters returned to Heaven,

and the fifty brothers were heartbroken,

except for Daleng and Yaleng,

now spending time deep in the cave.

With the sun rising and setting,

the moon waxing and waning,

Daleng and Yaleng had their sons and daughters,

and then generations multiplying and population flourishing.

When small caves were too crowded, they moved into big ones

until all caves on the earth were packed with people.

To ensure the survival of their descendants,

Yaleng and Daleng discussed about it carefully.

They cut bamboos and wood for the house frames and walls,

and collected thatches for the roof of the houses.

They brought birds, geese, and ducks from the waterway,

carried back pigs, cows, and sheep from the mountains,

and, when various plants yielded seeds to repay their kindness,

humans started to eat grains from then on.

Living the happy life today,

do not forget the ancestors' hard work.

The descendants of Daleng and Yaleng

filled up the flatlands and high mountains,

but they found, to praise the ancestors,

光靠嘴巴音调太简单。
种出葫芦做芦笙，
砍根青竹做吐良，
竹篾做出巧口弦，
掏空树心敲大鼓，
捏搓黄铜做出拔和铓，
世世代代把祖先的恩情歌唱。

河里有多少沙子，
人类就遇过多少魔鬼。
青树有多少叶子，
人类就受过多少苦难。
清平吉乐的世界，
气得妖魔发狂。
哈口气刮起黑风，
花木碎落鸟兽命丧，
翻江倒海山岳震撼，
要把大地的生命全部扫光。

一个人被吹出十里，
两个人被推出十丈。
一百个人抱成团，
气得风妖的胡须抖颤。
达楞和亚楞的子孙，
手拉手抱成几百团，
一团团冲向四面八方，

sing only with their mouths not enough.

They planted gourds to make Lusheng,

chopped green bamboo to make Tuliang,

peeled the bamboo skin to make mouth harps,

hollowed out the tree stems to make big drums,

compressed the brass to make cymbals and gongs,

so that the gratitude to the ancestors can be sung forever.

However many grains of the sand the rivers have,

that is the number of demons humans had encountered.

However many leaves the green trees have,

that is the number of disasters humans had suffered.

The peaceful and joyful world

drove the demons crazy.

With a breath, they blew the black wind,

which shattered flowers and trees, killed birds and beasts,

stirred up seas and rivers, shook up hills and mountains,

trying to sweep away all the life on the earth.

One person could be blown away for ten *li*,

but two people together were only pushed out for ten *zhang*.

Once a hundred people huddled together,

the demons' beard trembled with anger.

The descendants of Daleng and Yaleng,

hand in hand, huddled into hundreds of groups,

group by group, rushed in all directions,

把风妖撵进山洞赶下海洋。
人类要战胜一切妖魔，
必须依靠集体的力量。

人类在四面八方生长，
水土不同吃的不一样，
皮肉分黑白红黄，
说话有高低快慢。
同一祖先的人分成各民族，
各族人民都有一样的心肠。
各民族都用不同的歌舞，
把达古达楞的功绩颂扬。
各民族都是一个祖先传下，
亲弟兄要永远友爱互相帮忙。

种子撒进土里，
庄稼茁壮成长。
人类遍布大地，
到处鸟语花香。
各个民族都喝茶，
喝着苦水莫把祖宗忘。
未来的道路很远很远，
还会有魔鬼和苦难。
为了开拓新的生活，
《达古达楞格莱标》要贴在心口上。

until they drove the demons into the mountain caves and the
seas.

To defeat all demons,

humans must rely on the collective power.

As humans spread out in different places,

their diet varied from place to place,

their skin colors were of black, white, red, and brown,

and their speech featured high and low pitches, fast and
slow paces.

The same ancestors branched out into different nationalities,

but all ethnic groups have the same heart.

With different songs and dances,

they praise the achievements of Dagu and Daleng (ancestors).

All ethnic groups are descendants of the same ancestor,

all brothers should always love and help each other.

After seeds are sowed into the soil,

crops can thrive.

As humans are spread everywhere,

singing birds and sweet-scented flowers are everywhere.

All ethnic groups drink tea,

tasting the bitter tea and remembering the ancestors.

The future road is still long,

and there will be demons and sufferings.

For exploring the new life,

keep the *Earliest Dagu and Daleng Legends* close to your
heart.